the HALLS OF POWER

the HALLS OF POWER

a novel

by William C. Gordon

To Natalia Aguero

[signature] 2017

Bay Tree Publishing, LLC
Point Richmond, California

Calligraphy by Ward Schumaker
Cover design by Lori Barra and Sarah Kessler
Interior design by mltrees

Library of Congress Cataloging-in-Publication Data

Gordon, William C. (William Charles), 1937-
   The halls of power : a novel / by William C. Gordon.
      pages cm
   ISBN 978-0-9859399-3-9 (pbk. : alk. paper)
1. Reporters and reporting--California--San Francisco--Fic-tion. 2. Mystery fiction. 3. Noir fiction. I. Title.
   PS3607.O5947H35 2014
   813'.6--dc23
                                        2014005145

This book is dedicated to

Clive Matson, my writing teacher, who has

shepherded me through six novels.

Table of Contents

Part 1

1

The Accident?

It was late September 1963, and a busy morning at Conklin Chemical. The air was crisp and the sky clear and blue for as far as the eye could see.

In his office, Chad Conklin, the owner of the company, whistled cheerfully as he went over the delivery schedule with Sambaguita Poliscarpio, his Filipino director of operations. At six foot two, the trim and suntanned Conklin towered over his diminutive employee. They looked out the window of the company's building—located in the South of Market neighborhood, just off Third Street—onto the sparkling San Francisco Bay.

"We need to get that big holding tank cleaned out, and we have to hurry because they bring the bulk chemicals in at noon," Conklin told Sambaguita. "We have to mix and have the shipment ready by the day after tomorrow."

Sambaguita shook his head. "I don't think we can get it done that quick, Chief. There was a pretty nasty mixture in the big holding tank that left a lot of sludge that will have to be scooped out. We'll need to tilt the tank on its side before we can get a machine in there with an arm long enough to do the job, and we'll have to use the crane to tilt the tank."

"No, no, no," replied Conklin. "Send a man in there in the basket from the crane and he can fill the buckets with the sludge in just a couple of hours."

"I don't know, Chief. That's pretty toxic stuff. I don't think a man can do it by himself."

"Goddamn it, then send in two men with buckets instead of just one." Conklin laughed and turned away, shifting his attention to what else they'd need to do to get ready for the big delivery that was due at noon.

Still shaking his head, Sambaguita went out into the yard and sized up the fifteen-foot-high mixing tank. He went over to the crane operator and told him, "Lift me up in the basket so I can look into the tank."

The operator lowered the basket and Sambaguita climbed in and was hoisted to the top of the tank. He shined his power light into the four-foot opening and saw two feet of sludge at the bottom. As he sat in the basket, he calculated that it would take two men filling ten buckets each to scoop enough of the material out of the tank so it could be washed and drained. At the same time, he got a whiff of the noxious odor of the sludge. After ten seconds, the vapors made him so dizzy that he grew even more worried about the safety of his men.

"Okay, bring me down," he ordered.

When the basket was back on the ground, he went quickly back to the office. Conklin was busy with the bookkeeper, but Sambaguita interrupted them.

"It's too dangerous to send men down there. The fumes will kill them."

Conklin stood up to his full height and looked down at Sambaguita.

"Goddamn it, SP, I gave you an order. I want that tank ready by noon. Now get your ass out there and put two men in the tank, and I don't mean two jack-offs. Put the best men we have in there so the job is done right."

"I'm telling you, Chief, it's a bad situation. There is no ventilation."

"Bullshit!" Conklin fumed. "I'll take responsibility for this." He stomped out into the yard.

"Sanchez, come over here."

Roberto Sanchez, an illegal immigrant from Jalisco, Mexico—he was short and slim, with angular Indian cheekbones and intelligent brown eyes—was a whiz of a mechanic. He kept Conklin Chemical's complicated machinery humming, sometimes with bailing wire and tape. He stopped cleaning the hoses to a chemical tank and complied, coming to stand directly in front of Conklin. He, too, was small compared to the boss.

Conklin looked down into his handsome face. "You see that tank over there? Take one man and go in there with that bucket crane and clean it out by noon. *Comprende, amigo?*"

"*Sí señor*, I understand," said Roberto, who had listened carefully. He was always careful to listen to this boss and to comply with his wishes because the job was important to him and his family.

Conklin turned back to his director of operations. "Poliscarpio, get two ventilator masks from the tool shed."

Sambaguita went to the shed and made a quick study of the masks in the company's inventory, which were lined up against one of the walls. There were only five for the fifteen employees, and none of them had ever been used. Each had a rounded plastic enclosure with a leather strap that fit around the head of the worker. Attached to the plastic was a hose that led to a scuba-diver-like tank that had shoulder straps so it could be carried on the worker's back. He glanced at the expiration dates on the oxygen tanks and saw that they had all long passed their use-by dates.

He walked out of the shed and yelled to Conklin, "The air is dead in all of these."

"Let me see," Conklin demanded, running over. He took one mask and put it over his face, turning on the oxygen. It hissed, so he decided that it was functional.

"No need to worry, SP. I know from my Navy experience that these things last forever."

He handed two masks to Roberto, who by that time had called his cousin, Carlos Sanchez, over to help him.

"You put them on in the tank."

"*Sí señor,*" replied Roberto and Carlos.

They then made their way to the bucket of the crane with their equipment. They put on rubber boots and gloves, stacked several sludge buckets one inside another and climbed into the basket, which was about three feet deep. The crane operator lifted them up to the top of the tank. They stood in the middle of the basket, holding on to the cable. When it reached the opening of the tank, which was four feet in diameter, Carlos signaled the crane operator to center it over the opening.

Roberto and Carlos put on their respirator masks and were slowly lowered to the bottom of the tank. They looked at each other anxiously as they got out and began scooping the gunk into the sludge buckets with their shovels. The respirator masks were too tight to allow speech, but Carlos, in between his shoveling, kept pointing to his as if in distress. When full, each bucket was placed inside the basket by one of the two workers. Then Carlos pulled the cord and it was slowly lifted out of the tank, emptied of its cargo and returned to them. Carlos motioned to Roberto that they should work faster so they could get out of there.

They were filling the basket with buckets for the second time when Carlos keeled over. Roberto grabbed at him, but he couldn't keep him from falling facedown in the sludge. Roberto pulled him out of the sludge and yanked at the cord. The crane operator, thinking that the load was ready, hoisted the basket out of the tank, only to find it empty. Frantically, Roberto continued yanking on the line while trying to hold

Carlos up out of the sludge.

When Sambaguita saw the basket come to the top empty and registered the confused look on the crane operator's face, he realized there was a problem. "Get me up there fast," he yelled to the operator.

The operator quickly swung the basket down to the ground. Sambaguita grabbed a mask and motioned for the operator to lift him to the top of the tank. Before covering his mouth and nose with the ventilator mask, he yelled to a worker, "Call an ambulance and the fire department, tell them it's an emergency!" Then he ordered the crane driver to lower him into the tank. Once inside, he saw Roberto struggling to hold Carlos's limp, sludge-covered body out of the muck.

When Sambaguita reached the bottom of the tank, he grabbed at Carlos and tried to lift him, but his limp form slipped from his hands. He was finally able to grab Carlos by the arms even though his jacket was slimy with sludge, and, with the help of Roberto, threw the unconscious man over his shoulder. He then lowered Carlos into the basket, wedging his butt on the bottom with his arms and legs sticking up in the air. Sambaguita pulled on the cord, but at that instant his respirator mask failed and he inhaled the toxic fumes. He fainted, falling in a seated position back into the sludge.

Conklin came running from the office just as the basket came out of the tank holding a passed-out Carlos, his arms and his legs sticking out of the basket. Roberto was on the other side of the basket, retching and gasping for air. The operator shouted down to him that Sambaguita was still in the tank.

Acting quickly, Conklin singlehandedly removed Carlos and Roberto from the basket and laid them on the ground. He then grabbed one of the remaining masks and turned on the oxygen, but it didn't work. He threw the mask aside and gave the crane operator the signal to hoist him. When he was at the top, looking into the tank, he saw SP slouched, motionless, in the sludge.

Conklin's Navy training came back to him in a rush. "I want to be in and out of that tank in thirty seconds! Understand?"

The operator waved in acknowledgment, looked at his watch and lowered the bucket into the tank. Conklin held his breath.

As soon as the bucket splashed into the remaining sludge at the bottom of the tank, Conklin leapt out, grabbed Sambaguita and shook him, but there was no response. He lifted him into the basket, pulled the cord and they were hoisted up and out of the tank. The entire operation had taken less than the mandated thirty seconds. Conklin could breathe again, but tears were streaming down both cheeks from the toxic fumes.

Before they hit the ground, Conklin had ripped SP's mask off and was squeezing his belly rhythmically from behind. He pulled Sambaguita out of the basket, laid his body spread-eagled on the ground and kneeled over him, his hands working feverishly in rhythm against the unconscious man's diaphragm. SP began to stir as the hose man washed both men down, trying to rid them of the toxic sludge.

By the time the firemen arrived, the Conklin crew was working on Carlos, but it was too late. Roberto was shaking and continued to retch, his eyes still burning even though they had been washed.

Slowly Sambaguita came back to consciousness, but he, too, was having trouble breathing. Just as the ambulance attendants arrived to cart him away, Conklin leaned over and whispered in his ear. "Keep your mouth shut, Partner! You know nothing, understand? Remember, I saved your life, and I'll take care of everything. Just keep quiet."

* * *

The ambulance carrying Roberto and Sambaguita to the

respiratory unit at San Francisco General Hospital was pulling out just as Samuel Hamilton, a reporter for the city's morning newspaper, and Marcel Fabreceaux, his photographer, showed up in Marcel's green 1947 Ford. Marcel snapped a photograph of the ambulance as it sped off down the street. Before it left, one of the ambulance team members had used Conklin's office telephone to alert the medical examiner about the man they'd declared dead at the scene.

Samuel Hamilton got his start in the newspaper business by selling classified ads, but his investigation into the death of a friend of his, an apparent suicide, resulted in a major murder and smuggling case in Chinatown being solved. As a consequence, he'd been able to muscle his way into becoming a reporter. Since then he and Lieutenant Bruno Bernardi, a SFPD homicide detective, had worked together to solve other major homicide cases.

Even though he was shaken, Conklin knew how to keep things under control. While on his knees, still trying to revive Carlos, he'd seen in his peripheral vision Marcel taking his picture and Samuel with his notebook in hand.

Red-faced and still teary-eyed from the fumes, Conklin stood and turned toward Samuel, leaving his bookkeeper with the downed worker. "I'm trying to save a man's life here and you're all in the way, so get the fuck off my property!" He moved his broad-shouldered frame toward Samuel, Marcel and the two other reporters who had joined them.

"How about a statement about how this accident happened?" asked Samuel, seemingly unperturbed by man's aggressive stance. Marcel continued snapping photos of Conklin.

"You fuckers don't get it. This is my property and I want you off it, and I'm entitled to use force if necessary." He picked up a shovel and moved towards them. By the time he reached the chain-link gate, Samuel, Marcel and the other reporters had backed off. Conklin slammed the gate shut and locked it with the padlock.

"Read the paper tomorrow, you'll be in it," Samuel yelled after Conklin as the latter hurried to his office and slammed the door.

Ten minutes later, Lieutenant Bernardi of the SFPD homicide unit showed up with Philip Macintosh, his crime lab technician, and several other officers. Bernardi was a stocky five-foot-eight, with a wrestler's build and a flattened nose, a memento of his high school wrestling days. He was dressed in his usual drab brown suit, his hair cut short to match. As he got out of his 1960 black Ford Victoria, a blue police light stuck to the roof, Samuel approached him.

"Hi Bruno, you've got a real asshole in there. He's closed the gate and locked us out. I hope you came prepared for something like this."

Bernardi laughed. "Jesus Christ, Samuel, you always beat us to it. How do you do it?"

"I have a police band and I have a lot of friends," answered the reporter. "There must be a death here or you and Mac wouldn't have shown up."

"Yeah. That's what they tell me. Sounds like a chemical exposure, but we won't know until we get inside and take a look."

"We saw a man's body lying next to a tank, and it looked like people were working on him; tampering with evidence would be my guess. But that bastard pushed us out so quickly that I couldn't tell for sure what they were trying to hide. Unless you take me in with you, I'll have to wait until Marcel gets his pictures developed."

"You got photos of the body?" asked Bernardi.

"We think so," said Samuel. "Right, Marcel?"

"Yes, siree," said Marcel. "He looked pretty bad too."

"Can I publish it?" asked Samuel.

"You know the rules on these investigations, Samuel. First

we have to decide whether it can be used as evidence in a criminal case."

"Me publishing it in the paper won't prevent that," growled Samuel. "We were here before anybody else and we didn't tamper with a goddamned thing."

"All right. Just stay out of my way and don't touch anything," said the detective.

"Hey, you in there, open the gate," Bernardi yelled in a loud voice. "This is the SFPD and we're investigating a potential homicide." When he didn't get a response, he went back to his Ford Victoria and opened the trunk. He pulled out a battery-operated megaphone and returned to the gate.

"This is the San Francisco Police Department." His voice echoed loudly through the megaphone and onto the property. "If you don't unlock the gate, we'll break it down, as we have reason to believe that a crime has been or is being committed on these premises. And if we have to break down the fence, we'll arrest you for interfering with a police investigation. You have one minute to respond."

He put the megaphone down and winked at Samuel. Within the allotted minute, Conklin appeared from behind the building and sauntered towards the front gate. His blond hair was parted on one side and neatly combed. He had on dark sunglasses and was wearing a dark blue blazer with a Saint Francis Yacht Club insignia on the pocket.

"I'm sorry, Lieutenant. There were all kinds of trespassers coming in here—we were trying to save the poor man's life—I just had to keep the gate locked."

"Where is the man that is down?" asked Bernardi as Conklin unlocked the gate.

"I understand that the police have to do their work, but this is private property, and I don't want anyone who is not with your staff on the premises."

"Understood," said Bernardi, waving to Philip MacIntosh,

the crime scene technician, and the other police officers. They drove through the gate. Samuel tried to follow, but Conklin intervened.

"Not you, asshole." He slammed the gate shut and locked it again, then turned and caught up with Bernardi.

"I wouldn't lock the gate if I were you," said Bernardi. "The medical examiner is on his way and he doesn't like to be kept waiting."

"I'll open it just as soon as he gets here," said Conklin.

"You want to tell me what happened?"

"I've been instructed by my lawyer not to say anything," said Conklin.

"I'll make a note of that," said Bernardi. "Who's that man over there, leaning over the body?"

"That's my bookkeeper, and the man standing next to him is my crane operator."

"Okay, stand aside and don't get in my way."

"Can't I listen in on what you ask them?" asked Conklin, rubbing his hands on his pant legs and then crossing his arms in front of him.

"No. Since you've chosen silence, go to your office, if you have one, and we'll contact you when we're through."

"Wait a minute, this is my business. I have a right to listen in."

Bernardi called over a sergeant who had come with him. "Take this man to his office, and if he gives you any trouble handcuff him and take him down to the station."

"Yes, sir," said the sergeant, and he moved off with Conklin.

"I have a chemical shipment coming in at noon, and it's a big one," Conklin said over his shoulder. "I'll need to handle it." He rubbed his hands together and looked at his watch.

"You'll have to tell them to come back some other time. Right now, your premises are the site of a police investigation."

Conklin turned abruptly, stormed into his office and slammed the door.

Bernardi talked with one of his sergeants as they walked over to the mixing tank where Philip Macintosh was taking pictures of the body of the dead worker. "Keep an eye on Mister Big Shot, and if he uses the phone, make a note of the time and the length of the conversation so we can get information from Pacific Bell about who he was talking to."

When the medical examiner arrived, Conklin rushed to the gate and unlocked it. The examiner made his way to the accident site, where Bernardi was waiting.

"Hi Barney," said Bernardi, saluting him.

"What have we here?" asked Barney McLeod, a tall, slender Irishman with thinning brown hair. He was affectionately known as "Turtle Face" because of his long neck and the fact that he never smiled.

"From the looks of it," said Bernardi, "he was overcome inside the tank. I was just going to question the crane operator."

"I saw your buddy outside."

"You mean Samuel?"

"The one and only," said the examiner. "You two are usually inseparable. What happened?"

"The owner wouldn't let him in. He must have heard of his reputation."

Barney laughed. "A real bulldog, alright. A true crimefighter."

They walked together to where the body of Carlos Sanchez lay. Although he was covered with slime from the tank, his face was clean. The examiner studied the dead man's contorted face. "Someone cleaned him up. He should have green bile running from his mouth and his nose, and his eyes should be staring blankly into space."

"Samuel's man got some photos of Conklin hovering over the body."

"I need to talk with him. Maybe he caught him in the act of cleaning up the body. That's a crime." He motioned for his photographer to get pictures of the man's face and head.

"Nice-looking young man, probably pretty healthy until today." He pulled a small mirror from the vest pocket of his white lab coat and placed it over the nose and mouth of the victim. It didn't cloud up. Next, he took out his stethoscope and checked for a heartbeat. There was none. Then he knelt down on one knee and examined his eyes. "From the broken blood vessels that show in the whites of his eyes, it looks like he was poisoned, probably from the fumes in the tank. You know that smell, don't you, Lieutenant?" Then he gently closed the dead man's eyelids.

"Can't say that I do," said Bernardi.

"It's like the cyanide concoction they use in the gas chamber over at San Quentin to execute condemned killers."

Bernardi bit his lip and shook his head. "Poor bastard, he got the sentence, but his only crime was coming to California for a better economic future."

Turtle Face shrugged. "You have a point there," he said. He waved his men over. "All right, boys, load him up.

"I'll be out of your way in ten minutes, Lieutenant. Let me know what the witnesses say. I'll hold off on the cause of death until I hear from you. If you can't give me a clear cause and effect, I may have to have an inquest."

His men zipped the body into a body bag, placed it on a gurney and rolled it to the medical examiner's vehicle, where it was loaded into the back. They drove to the front gate and honked the horn. Conklin came out of his office and unlocked the gate. The vehicle drove out and stopped directly in front of Samuel, who was frantically waving his arms.

As the examiner got out, he was almost laughing. "You

again, Samuel? It's gotta be ESP. I want to see the photos Marcel took. Someone cleaned the dead guy up."

"How did you know we had photos?"

"I was told you got it on film, or the owner wouldn't have kicked you out."

Samuel was still fuming from being ordered off the property, but he began to laugh, too. "That's how you knew what I was going to tell you." As a result of Barney's statement, he stopped feeling that he had been shut out of what he considered an important story. Judging from Conklin's treatment of him, as well as his posturing, the reporter had already decided that the man was hiding something important and was worthy of an exposé. Samuel knew by now that he had some power as a reporter, and that people like Conklin feared him.

"We did get some photographs of the owner and someone else working on the man while he was down. They'll be in tomorrow morning's paper. Other than that, I'm not sure. I'll have to go over the photographs to see if there was something else I picked up that bothered the S.O.B." Samuel spoke in an extra-loud voice, within earshot of Conklin, who once again slammed the gate and rushed back to his office.

"Okay, Samuel. Make sure I get copies of those photographs. Why not come by the office and we'll talk about this? In the meantime, I'll perform the autopsy and we can compare notes."

"Sure thing, Barney. I'll call you tomorrow. You know about the two guys in the hospital, don't you? I'll go over there this afternoon and see if I can interview them. But I'll have to use Bernardi's muscle to get in to see them."

Back at the site, Bernardi questioned the crane operator. He told him that the two workers he'd pulled out of the tank were unconscious, and that when the foreman followed them down into the tank, he'd come up unconscious too.

Then Bernardi and the crane operator examined the

oxygen tanks lying on the ground, noting that their expiration dates had passed. "How do we get the three oxygen tanks that are in the tank?" asked Bernardi.

"Either you send you own men in there or we tip the tank over and get a grappling hook to pull them out of the sludge."

"I think that's the way to go," agreed Bernardi. He turned to his crime scene technician. "Mac, get photos of the status quo and then get your men to tip the tank over and we'll follow this man's advice and fish them out."

They all left the shed and walked over to the tank. "Can you lift one of my men up in that basket?" Bernardi asked the crane operator. "We'll put a cable around the lip of that tank and use the crane to tip it over."

"Sure can," said the operator.

A police officer holding an extra cable climbed in the basket. After being hoisted to the top of the tank, he looped the cable around the lip and tied it securely.

When the tank was on its side, Mac extracted the gooey masks from the muck with a grappling hook. A cursory glance at each tag revealed that the air had expired on all of them. "This looks pretty bad," he said, placing each of the masks in a separate box.

Conklin came out of his office and put on his dark glasses. "My load of chemicals will be here in a half an hour," he said, nervously looking at his watch. "I need to get the men ready to receive it."

"We should be through by then, but if we're not, your shipment will just have to wait, Mr. Conklin. By the way, how many employees do you have?"

Conklin walked back into his office without answering and slammed the door. Bernardi turned toward the man who had been identified as the bookkeeper. "I guess it's up to you, then. How many?"

"We have fifteen laborers plus the foreman, me and the boss."

"That's eighteen altogether, and there are only five respirator masks. Is that correct?"

"That's not my department. You'll have to ask Mr. Poliscarpio. He's the foreman."

"Isn't that one of the fellows they took to the hospital?"

"Yes, sir."

When he was ready to leave, Bernardi called over the sergeant who had been watching Conklin in the office. "Did he make any calls?"

"Yes, sir. A couple. One lasted more than ten minutes."

"Okay, we'll have to get the phone number from Pacific Bell." Bernardi smiled wryly at the sergeant. "Not a very pleasant chap, is he?"

"No, sir," answered the sergeant. "He has a chip on his shoulder."

"Let's see if we can knock it off," said Bernardi.

* * *

Samuel and the two patrolmen assigned to him by Lieutenant Bernardi arrived at the San Francisco General Hospital respiratory ward shortly after noon, and Samuel told the nurse at the desk that he wanted to see Robert Sanchez and Sambaguita Poliscarpio.

"Are you a family member?"

"No, this is police business."

"Very well," said the nurse. "I need to see your authorization,"

Samuel handed her his press ID and the patrolmen gave her their shields. She studied the ID's briefly before handing them back and dutifully wrote each of their names down in the journal at her desk. The nurse then got up and perused the admitting notebook. After a minute or so, she returned to her desk. "I have a record of Mr. Sanchez, but I have none for Mr. Poliscarpio."

"You're kidding, I saw the ambulance leave with Mr. Poliscarpio in it."

"That may be, but he wasn't brought here." She took Samuel over to the notebook and showed him.

"Jesus Christ," he stammered, furrowing his brow. "I need to use your phone."

She pointed to her desk, and Samuel rushed over and dialed Bernardi's number. The secretary who answered told him Bernardi was at lunch.

"This is Samuel Hamilton. Tell him I'm at General Hospital and that one of the injured workers is missing."

He called out to the nurse who'd been helping him and handed her the phone. "Will you give the secretary this number so the lieutenant can return my call?"

After the nurse put down the phone, Samuel presented her with another request. "I need to find out what ambulance company brought Mr. Sanchez to the hospital."

"Go down to emergency. They can tell you."

"What about Sanchez? Is he conscious?"

"Not yet. He's on a respirator. The doctor said no one could talk to him until tomorrow."

"Okay. Don't let anyone in to see him until I get back with Lieutenant Bernardi. I'll leave Patrolman Sullivan here to make sure. Understood?"

"Yes, sir. I'll leave instructions for the night shift."

Samuel took the elevator to the first floor and walked down the hall to the emergency room with the second officer that Bernardi had assigned to him. The admitting room reeked of vomit and was full-to-overflowing with the flotsam and jetsam of San Francisco: the poor and uninsured and those who had been scraped off its back streets and pulled from its darkest corners. There were several gurneys in the hallway and nurses and attendants ran from one patient to the next with IV bottles and stethoscopes, checking to see who was still alive and could be moved to a ward to make room for new arrivals.

Samuel approached the admitting desk and asked the nurse in charge—a big, busty woman with bleached blond hair wearing horn-rimmed glasses—if she could help locate a patient who had been brought into Emergency by an ambulance around noon.

"What was the patient's name and where did he come from?" she asked, looking over the top of her glasses and ignoring the ringing phone.

"He came from Conklin Chemical Company down by the bay, South of Market. I believe his name was Sambaguita Poliscarpio. Does that ring a bell?"

She looked in her admitting records and shook her head. "We have no record of your Mr. Poliscarpio being admitted to San Francisco General Hospital today."

"We know that, ma'am. Can you tell us which ambulance driver brought in Mr. Roberto Sanchez so we can ask him what happened to the other patient who was with him."

The nurse looked at Sanchez's intake record. "Yes, I should have that."

"What ambulance driver brought him in?"

She looked again. "Actually, it doesn't say. It's blank. See what they have in operations. Go out the door and you'll find it. I've done everything I can for you." She slammed the cover of her intake journal binder closed and picked up the ringing phone.

The operations desk was in a small office next to the emergency room. When Samuel and the police officer walked in, a tired-looking man dressed in a wrinkled white uniform was clearly losing the battle with three phones that never stopped ringing.

"We're trying to locate a patient who arrived in an ambulance a couple of hours ago, but who's not registered at the hospital."

"Good luck, Mister. We get twenty ambulances an hour coming in here. I don't even have time to keep track of them. They put their paperwork in that pile. If you can find a record of it coming in, you can find out who the driver was." He pointed to the mass of papers stuck on a single spike.

Samuel shuffled through the pile until he found the paperwork for a pick-up at Conklin Chemical shortly after eleven in the morning. "Here it is, but there's no ambulance number or driver's name on it. Is there any other way to tell what was the ambulance number or who the driver was?"

"Let's see," said the harried dispatcher. "You can wait around all afternoon and ask the drivers as they come in if they remember the pick-up, or you can go to the patient's record and that will give you the name. Other than that, you're shit out of luck."

Samuel motioned to the patrolman. "Let's go back up to the ward and see if we can talk to the other witness."

The asked the nurse with the bleached blond hair and horn-rimmed glasses if they could speak to Roberto Sanchez, but she informed them that he'd been transferred to intensive care, and was under doctor's orders not to have any visitors.

"Where is intensive care? Is there a chance he'll die?"

"If he's in intensive care, there's always a chance he can die. You go up two floors and follow the arrows. You'll find it. But you'd better talk to Doctor Malakoff. He's in charge of the patient."

Samuel and the officer reached intensive care, where they encountered Officer Sullivan and a nurse with a big hairdo and a snotty attitude. "We're here from the police department to talk with Roberto Sanchez. Is Doctor Malakoff around?"

"No, sir," said the nurse. "He makes his rounds early in the morning, so come back then."

Samuel tried to explain that there had been a potential homicide, and that he needed to talk to the witness to get information.

"That's not my concern, Mister. What is your name anyway?"

"My name is Samuel Hamilton. This is Officer Sullivan and Officer Martin. It's their job to guard the witness so that no one other than the police or their representatives get in to talk with him. Do I need to have the head of Homicide show up to make my point about how important this is?"

The nurse came down off her high horse a little. "Sorry, Mr. Hamilton, as you can tell, this place is a madhouse. I'll get Doctor Malakoff on the phone and you can talk to him."

"I need to see the patient's record."

She went to her desk but it wasn't there. "I'll have to retrieve it from outside his room. Give me a minute."

She returned with Sanchez's chart. "Does it say who transported him from the chemical factory?"

"Unfortunately, it wasn't signed."

"Does it say what ambulance he came in?"

"Not even that, I'm afraid. Why don't you try dispatch again? Maybe he will recognize the handwriting."

"Can I borrow this for a couple of minutes?"

"Be my guest," said the nurse.

Samuel took the sheet downstairs, but the dispatcher was unable to identify the handwriting. Ten minutes later, he was on the phone with Dr. Malakoff, who advised him that the patient was too fragile to question and that he should discuss the matter the next morning with the doctor on call.

Samuel dialed Bernardi's number, and this time the detective was in. "You'd better get some help for Officer Sullivan and Officer Martin. It doesn't sound to me like this witness is going to be in any shape to talk to us for a few days. I'll have to do some work to find out what happened to this Poliscarpio guy, but I think I have a way to find out which ambulance driver brought him in."

"Should I put out an all-points bulletin for him?" asked Bernardi.

"That wouldn't hurt. On the other hand, he's probably not out in the open somewhere. Let me follow a hunch and I'll get back to you later this afternoon."

"Okay. Give the phone to Sullivan, and just in case I forget, tell him not to leave until I make arrangements to have a team replace them."

Samuel called the officer over. "Bernardi wants to talk to you. He said not to leave until he had a team here to replace you."

"I've got to get out of here," Samuel told Sullivan after the officer finished his conversation with Bernardi and hung up. "Remember, don't allow anyone in to see Sanchez unless Bernardi approves. I'll call you later just to check. Whatever you do, don't let the Conklin guy in to to see him."

After giving the officer Conklin's full name and physical description, Samuel pondered the situation. He'd been shut out from what he considered an important story because the company owner recognized him as an aggressive reporter. This bothered him. At the same time, he knew that something was really wrong. Conklin's behavior was a big enough clue for him to put all his effort into investigating him.

* * *

Samuel and Marcel sat in the morning paper's photo lab, going over the pictures the photographer had taken at Conklin Chemical earlier that day.

"Here it is," said Samuel excitedly, taking a drink from his cup of lukewarm coffee. "This is the ambulance that picked them up. There's a number on that ambulance. Can you enlarge that photo so I can read the number correctly and make out the license plate?"

"Yeah, but it'll take me about a half hour."

"Okay," said Samuel as he shuffled through the other photos on the desk. "While you're at it I also want you to enlarge these photos of Conklin leaning over the man on the ground there, wiping his face with that cloth. You see what I mean? There are at least three of them. I want to use one for my article in tomorrow's paper."

"Which do you want first? It's all a matter of priorities."

"Identifying the ambulance by getting the number and the license plate is the most important thing right now. No one else has these photos, so Conklin has no idea we can trace the witness. Bernardi is going to be both very happy and very pissed off that this jerk is screwing around with a witness and that he doctored the evidence."

Samuel got on the phone and told Bernardi what he had.

"Good work. Get me the number and the license plate and we'll get in touch with the dispatcher and the Department of Motor Vehicles in Sacramento right away. You and I can interview the driver."

"It may not be that easy. They have twenty ambulances and it's going to require some digging."

"When we confirm the ambulance number, we'll find the guys who were driving it this morning. We can do that right away. Get back to me as soon as you have it."

* * *

Within the hour, Bernardi and Samuel were at the ambulance barn at San Francisco General Hospital, looking for an ambulance marked No. 5 with the license plate E 723145—the identifiers that had shown up in Marcel's enlarged photo.

When they found an ambulance with those plates, they confirmed that the number "5" was painted on its roof and back door. Bernardi walked into the operations office, showed the clerk his badge and gave him the information.

"We need to talk to the driver of No. 5, which made a pick-up earlier today at Conklin Chemical, and we want any paperwork you have on it."

The employee shuffled through the papers that had been removed from the spike. When he found what he was looking for, he handed a sheet of paper to Bernardi.

"How come you couldn't find that earlier today?" asked Samuel.

"Because you didn't tell me the number five."

"Where can we find this ambulance driver?" asked Bernardi.

The dispatcher looked at his employee sheet. "He went home at three o'clock."

"Give us his full name, address and a phone number," said Bernardi.

The dispatcher rummaged in his drawer and took out a small personal phone book. "Here it is," he said, scribbling the information on a piece of paper. "He's one of the reliable ones. His name is Milford Jackson and he lives up on Fillmore. Do you want me to call him and tell him you're coming to see him?"

"That's exactly what I want you to do," said Bernardi. "Tell him we'll be there in twenty minutes and not to leave before we get there."

The dispatcher made the call and advised Bernardi that Jackson was waiting for him.

Bernardi and Samuel got to the Fillmore address quickly and rang Mr. Jackson's doorbell. He answered immediately.

"I'm Lieutenant Bernardi. This is Mr. Hamilton. We need to talk with you."

"Milford Jackson at your service, Lieutenant," said the man, a tall, thin Negro with short-cropped hair, sharp cheekbones and an aquiline nose.

"You brought two injured parties to the hospital earlier today from Conklin Chemical," said Bernardi. "We know where Mr. Sanchez is, but we can't find the other man who was in the ambulance with him. What happened to him?"

Jackson looked startled. "Am I in trouble, Lieutenant?"

"No, no, nothing like that. We're investigating a case, is all. The other injured party disappeared. We need to know where he went."

"It was kinda weird," said Jackson. He spoke with a soft Southern drawl. "When we drove up to the emergency entrance, there were two attendants from another ambulance company waiting for us. They showed me some I.D. and told me that they had been called on behalf of Conklin Chemical to pick up one of the two people in the ambulance. I'm sorry, I can't recollect the gentleman's name."

"Sambaguita Poliscarpio?"

The driver's eyes widened with recognition. "That's the name, the Filipino guy." He paused and thought for a few seconds. "They signed my pick-up sheet. Right there, see?" He pointed to the paper Bernardi had in his hand. "They transferred him to a gurney, put him in their ambulance and took off."

"What was the name of the company they worked for?" asked Samuel.

"You know, the ambulance didn't have a name on it, but it was white and it definitely was an ambulance," said Jackson.

"Did you recognize either of the attendants?" asked Samuel.

He shook his head. "I've never seen neither of them before. That's all I know."

Samuel saw that they weren't going to get anything more

from Jackson, so he nudged Bernardi, indicating it was time to move on.

As they left the driver's house, Samuel's mind was working overtime. "There has to be a way to trace that ambulance."

"I'll put somebody on it as soon as I get back to the office," said Bernardi. "But Christ, there must be five hundred ambulance companies in the Bay Area."

"What about getting hold of Conklin's phone records? He must have been the one who called them."

"Yeah, my man already told me he was on the phone. That's on my list of things to get moving on first thing in the morning."

"Okay. I'm headed for Camelot. Want to join me for a drink?"

"Not today. Too much work to do. Let's talk tomorrow. Good work on finding the ambulance driver."

"I'd hardly call that good work. That bastard Conklin is one step ahead of us."

"The odds are pretty good that that won't last long. He'll fuck up. They always do."

"I think he already has," said Samuel. "But let's see just how nasty he gets before we expose him for what he is."

* * *

Samuel left the newspaper's Market Street office and walked past the Emporium department store toward Powell, where he hopped on the Hyde Street Cable Car. He rode it up to Nob Hill and jumped off right in front of Camelot, his favorite watering hole, which overlooked a park and the San Francisco Bay. It had been a long day and he was tired.

Seated just inside the door at a large, circular oak table—Samuel always thought of it as the Round Table—was Melba, the middle-aged owner, who was well known for her blue-tinted hair. She could usually be found sipping a beer and smoking a Lucky Strike cigarette with Excalibur, her faux Airedale mutt with a missing ear and tail, lying on the floor next to her. This day was no exception.

When the dog sensed Samuel walk in, he leapt up in excitement, looking for the treat the reporter always had for him. Melba pulled on his leash to restrain him but he put his paws up on the table and licked Samuel's hands until the reporter produced the treat.

"Where in the hell have you been, Samuel? I haven't seen you since you and my daughter shacked up."

Samuel blushed but said nothing.

"I see. The strong, silent type, huh? Well, goddamn it, I want a grandchild. So you'd better start working overtime."

"Speaking of your daughter, she told me she'd be back from Tahoe tomorrow. Have you heard anything from her?"

"Nowadays you seem to know more about her than I do," laughed Melba. "Are you sure you'll be able to handle her? You look worn out. What happened?"

Samuel did have a bedraggled look. His khaki sports coat was wrinkled and his shirt was untucked. "It's been a rough one," he said and proceeded to explain what his day had been like.

"Chad Conklin, huh?" said Melba when Samuel finished talking. "That boy got lucky when he nabbed Grace Abernathy. Her old man is worth millions."

"Really?" said Samuel. "You know who he is? I can't believe it. Did someone else write an article about him before I got to press?"

"Nah. He's a San Francisco story. Conklin's an Okie from Bakersfield. His family comes from the Dust Bowl. If he hadn't been a football star at Cal, he'd never have nabbed that little dish. But she's not exactly top drawer herself. Her father's a nouveau riche Irishman who made a ton of money in the scrap iron business."

"How in the hell do you know all this, Melba?"

She laughed and took a swig of her beer. "Shit, Samuel. You think I sit here on my ass all day doing nothing? Wrong!" She stood up and placed her hands on her waist. "First, I read the gossip columns. I know where every piss ant comes from, including you. That means I know how they got where they think they are.

"All these fuckers have enemies. Some of their worst ones bend their elbows at my bar. When a name is mentioned I prick up my ears and listen. Then I ask questions. So what do you want to know about this asshole?"

"Jesus, Melba. You're kind of the answer to a prayer. I'll come back tomorrow with my notebook. Right now, I need a drink."

2

Another San Francisco Power Struggle or Something More Sinister?

THE NEXT DAY, THE MORNING paper headline screamed:

Millionaire Industrialist Concealed
Evidence, Hid Critical Witness

The byline was Samuel Hamilton, and the article took Conklin head on. The reporter wanted Conklin to know that he had an adversary who wouldn't take any shit from him. The article included a photograph of Chad Conklin wiping the face of the deceased worker, Carlos Sanchez, and it left no doubt of the reporter's belief that Conklin was behind the disappearance of his injured foreman, Sambaguita Poliscarpio.

The response was swift and aggressive. The biggest and most important law firm in the city hand-delivered a letter to the newspaper publisher demanding the article be retracted and the reporter fired. It also threatened a lawsuit for libel if those demands were not carried out immediately.

Summoned for a meeting with the editor-in-chief, Samuel entered the wood-paneled office tentatively, not sure what to expect. The editor, overweight and balding, stood up from behind his large desk and waved the morning paper in the air. He was sweating profusely, even though it was not a hot day. "You'd better have the goods on this bastard or we're ruined!" he shouted. "Do you hear me?"

Taken by surprise, Samuel frowned. "What are you talking about, Chief?"

"This goddamned letter that was hand-delivered to me just before noon," the editor stammered, tossing it at Samuel.

The reporter picked up the scattered pages from the floor and sat down to read them carefully. As he did, he grimaced and uttered curses beneath his breath. When he'd finished, he looked up at his boss quizzically. "Isn't truth a defense to a libel claim?"

"You're goddamned right it is, after we've spent a hundred thousand dollars to defend your right to print whatever the fuck you want to. They also demand that I fire you. What do you say to that?"

"I think the same thing I did before I wrote the article: that truth is a defense to this kind of bullshit. And you can't let these assholes intimidate you."

"That's easy for you to say, you don't pay the bills," said the fat man, using his handkerchief to wipe the sweat off his face.

"I went over all this with you before it went to press and you approved it." Samuel was starting to get angry. "You saw the photos and read the article, didn't you? Do you think I had my head up my ass?"

"I don't know, I don't know. What I do know is that the publisher is going to want answers. Are you prepared to give them to him?"

"Of course, I am. Don't you want to hear them too?"

"Save your breath. I'm not the one you have to convince. The publisher wants to see you tomorrow morning." The editor-in-chief put his now-wet handkerchief on the ink blotter of his desk.

The Halls of Power

* * *

Samuel rushed to Bernardi's office to go over the evidence his men had collected at the accident site. He knew that he'd gone out on a limb in the article by saying that Conklin was behind the disappearance of a material witness, but he felt that no one besides Conklin could be responsible. He could live with his decision to make that statement public. But he wanted to know what the lieutenant or his men had found out about it since the day before.

After learning there was nothing new, he walked over to the medical examiner's office for his meeting with Turtle Face. "Hi Barney," he said, his face grim.

"What the hell's bothering you?" asked the examiner, who was seated beside a real human skeleton that hung next to his office blackboard. On the other side of the blackboard was his gallery of celebrity photos.

"Conklin and his lawyers are threatening to sue me is all," said the reporter, his lower lip protruding.

Turtle Face laughed. "Don't you know you're not considered a real man in this town until you've been sued at least five times?"

"That's no consolation. You're a public servant. I work for a private company and Conklin wants me fired too." Samuel studied his scuffed shoes and let out a sigh.

"The hell you say. Come work for me. You're a great investigator, and from what I've heard, you'll get better pay."

Samuel laughed. Barney made him feel better—and he was right. Being a public servant probably would pay better than being a hack reporter, but that was what he loved doing, so he wasn't about to change of his own accord.

"Thanks, Barney…Let's get down to business. You saw the photo in the morning paper. I have that one and two more of Conklin wiping the dead man's face."

"That's good," said the examiner. "I also understand from Bernardi that the masks that were supposed to contain oxygen were empty. The expiration dates on all of them were long past. That means it could be decided that death was caused by means other than accident."

"Who has the power to decide that?" asked Samuel.

"It's not simple," said Turtle Face. "I have to hold an inquest and it really depends on the evidence that comes out during the hearing."

"Who's the judge at such a hearing?"

Turtle Face's expression showed that he was more than a bit insulted. "I am." He folded his arms across his chest. "And you can count on one thing for sure. I call 'em the way I see 'em. And it's all based on the evidence."

"What happens if you decide that death was caused by some other means than an accident?"

"Then it's up to the D.A."

Samuel felt a little better, secure in the knowledge that Barney McLeod was neither a bullshitter nor subject to outside influence. He also knew that the D.A. would prosecute his own mother if he thought he could get a conviction.

"Wasn't there some public entity that was supposed to make periodic inspections of that facility?" asked Samuel.

"I have someone looking into that right now. I'll have more on it by the end of the week. It will be interesting to see why they had the masks in the first place, if they never checked them to see if they worked."

"It could have been for eyewash," said Samuel. "You know, just to show them off when people come around, so they could claim they make the place safe for their employees, when in fact it's all bullshit, just a public relations ploy."

"They wouldn't be the first, would they?" said Turtle Face.

* * *

Samuel spent a sleepless night at his small apartment on the edge of Chinatown. After a quick cappuccino and croissant at Café Trieste, he presented himself outside the newspaper publisher's office at the appointed time, wearing a pressed khaki sports coat and shined penny loafers. A secretary announced him. Some ten minutes later, a tall man with gray hair parted to one side came through a large mahogany double door. The publisher shook his hand vigorously and invited Samuel into the inner sanctum.

"Have a seat, Mr. Hamilton. Looks like we're in for a rough ride, doesn't it?" He surprised the reporter by not wasting time on chitchat.

"I'm not a forecaster of the future, sir," Samuel answered. "But I'll tell you, I think we've done the right thing by exposing this bastard. He's just too big for his britches and the only way to handle someone like him is to stand up and call his bluff." Samuel had not expected to be so straightforward with the paper's owner, but his was a spontaneous response to the man's directness. After all, Samuel reasoned, he had the perfect solution: expose Conklin for what he was.

"We like you here, Mr. Hamilton," said the publisher. "In the short time you've been a reporter for this newspaper, you've worked very well for us. You've developed good sources and given the public and us what we wanted—exciting and interesting stories." He clasped his hands together. "But my responsibilities are also to the shareholders, and they don't like getting threatening letters from the city's powers-that-be, claiming that they have been falsely accused. As it stands now, we are going to have to engage a legal team to defend you and the paper. So I'm going to have to put you on furlough, regretfully without pay. I'm sorry."

Dumbfounded, Samuel stood up. The tension in the room was thick as the two men stared at each other in silence. "Is that it?" Samuel finally blurted once he had recovered from the initial shock. "You've got to be kidding. I have the goods on this guy. His lawsuit is a charade. It won't hold water. It will be kicked out of court, if it even gets that far." The reporter pounded his fist on the expensive desk. "What about freedom of the press? What about my rent?" He added the second question as an afterthought, but he could see that the meeting was over, and soon found himself out on the street with zero income.

* * *

It was only nine in the morning—Camelot wasn't open yet—so Samuel stopped at the corner liquor store. He bought a pack of Philip Morris cigarettes and ripped the aluminum foil off. Just like in the old days, he tapped the package until a cigarette came out, put it in his mouth, lit it and took a deep drag. The first inhalation made him dizzy and he reached out to hold onto the counter. Samuel knew it was a stupid idea to start smoking again, but he didn't give a shit. He was out of a job and he was depressed.

He walked outside to Market Street, sat down on a bench at the bus stop and smoked his cigarette, looking up at the Ferry Building clock. When it struck ten, he got up and walked back up the street until he got to Powell. He considered hopping on the next cable car, which would deliver him in front of Camelot in fifteen minutes, but realized the bar still wouldn't be open yet. It would be better to kill time by walking there instead. He headed up Powell towards Nob Hill.

Almost a half an hour later Samuel stood in front of the bar, sweating and breathing heavily from the long climb. The bar still wasn't open so he walked across the street and sat down on a bench in the park overlooking the bay and had another smoke. After finishing his cigarette, he threw the pack in the trashcan. The last thing he needed was to take up smoking again.

When Camelot finally opened at eleven, he went in and ordered a double Scotch on the rocks, which he quickly downed. Five drinks later, he stumbled back to the park to look in the trashcan for the pack he'd thrown away, but it was gone. He went back to Camelot, put a quarter in the cigarette machine and got another pack of Philip Morris smokes. By that time Melba had shown up, Excalibur in tow. The dog jumped up and down in excitement but Samuel, smoking a cigarette, ignored him. Melba used the leash to restrain her dog and studied Samuel closely.

"You'd better go home and sleep this one off," she said. "Come back tonight or tomorrow and we'll have a man-to-man talk."

Samuel walked unsteadily over to the Round Table and tried to say something, but he couldn't get the words out. He slid into a chair, put his head down between his arms and fell into a snoring sleep. About an hour later he woke up and looked around, disoriented. When he saw Melba sitting quietly at the other end of the table sipping a beer, he shook his head, got up and walked out the door, too drunk to care what anyone thought of him, and stumbled down the sidewalk to his apartment. Climbing into his Murphy bed, he promptly fell back to sleep.

It was half past noon the following day when Samuel woke up again, this time with a splitting headache. He sat on the edge of his bed and lit a cigarette, then got up and went to the refrigerator for a bottle of Hamm's. After opening it, he downed the beer in one long gulp. Stripping off his undershirt and shorts, Samuel took a shower, but he didn't bother shaving. He got dressed again and went up the street to Camelot, heading straight for the horseshoe-shaped bar. "I'll have the usual."

"What's that?" asked the bartender, who was new and

didn't know him.

"It's a double Scotch on the rocks, lad. Get used to this face, you'll see a lot of it."

He was well into his second drink when Melba and Excalibur entered the bar through the back door. She flinched when she saw Samuel hunched over the bar smoking a cigarette. "He's eighty-sixed!" she yelled across to the bartender.

Samuel turned around, startled. "Come on Melba, I need a crutch. I just got fired."

"Don't bullshit me, cowboy. You're just feeling sorry for yourself. And you're well on your way to hell in a hand basket." She took the reporter by the arm and steered him to the Round Table. "Sit here and have a cup of coffee. Here's the morning paper—read the front page and weep." Melba placed her hands on her hips. "But I have news for you, and I think it's going to help."

Samuel skimmed the front page. Front and center was a retraction of the article he'd written two days before. "Those bastards! They know that fucker is lying. How can they do that? I'm ashamed to be a reporter."

"They're trying to cover their asses. That's why I want you to meet Jim Abernathy."

Samuel looked up, shocked. "You mean the father of Conklin's wife?"

"The same. I was talking to him the other day after your article came out, and he said he wanted to meet with you. And it isn't to defend Conklin, you'll be happy to know. So finish your coffee, go home, take a nap, shave and be back here at five this afternoon. And bring my goddamned dog a treat, will you? His feelings are hurt."

"You bet," said Samuel, getting up and wobbling out the door. Even though he was still weaving as he walked down the sidewalk, he felt a bounce return to his step.

3

Jim Abernathy

When Samuel walked into Camelot later that day, a well-dressed man was sitting at the Round Table with Melba. They were both smoking cigarettes, and one of them must have just told a joke because they were both howling with laughter. The man looked to be in his early fifties. He had thick gray hair, a nose as straight as a line of type, piercing blue eyes and a craggy face that had seen too much sun.

Samuel looked like his old self again, though he now had a new and determined glint in his eye. Since he'd left Camelot earlier in the day, he'd soaked up his hangover with lunch at his favorite bargain-basement restaurant, Chop Suey Louie's.

He'd also remembered Melba's parting words—that he shouldn't forget his most loyal fan—so he took a treat out of his pocket and gave it to the ever-appreciative Excalibur, who wolfed it down in one gulp.

"Samuel, say hello to Jim Abernathy," said Melba. "He's read all your articles and asked to meet with you."

Samuel shook the most rough and calloused hand he had ever felt. Placing his half-full pack of Philip Morris cigarettes on the table, he slid it across to Melba. "Here's a few smokes for you."

"I don't smoke those particular cancer sticks," she said,

pulling out a pack of Lucky Strikes. "Give them to the bartender. I think that's his brand."

"I'll check that out before I leave," said Samuel, turning his attention to Abernathy. "It's a pleasure to meet you, sir. I only know of you through Melba. You have heard of my circumstances, as you no doubt read the paper."

"Yes, lad," Abernathy said in a distinct Irish brogue. He was friendly but reserved. "When I read the article you wrote I called Melba 'cause methinks I can help ya with some background."

"Isn't your daughter married to Chad Conklin?"

"That's so, and a miserable bastard he is," Abernathy said forcefully, though Samuel detected a natural reserve behind the words.

"I'll be honest with you, Mr. Abernathy. I understand you're a very wealthy man. Most people of your ilk don't get there by being nice guys, so you obviously want me to print something in the newspaper that kicks him in the ass or settles a grudge you have with him. I have two problems with that. As you can see from today's paper, and as you've no doubt heard from Melba, I no longer have a platform to speak from." Samuel stood to emphasize his point, his hands pressed against the oak of the Round Table. "Second, I worry about being used as an instrument to get even."

"Listen, young fella. Don't worry about that. You'll soon be back on top. And you're right. I have my grievances against what you Americans call this gold digger. He is a lying sack of shit and I'm gonna be your informant by giving you a lot of inside dope that will help you get to the bottom of his bag of tricks." Abernathy extracted a Philip Morris from Samuel's discarded pack and lit it.

"What are you doing?" asked Melba in mock horror.

"One's as good as another," he said. "They'll all kill ya." He inhaled deeply before continuing. "And with my influence—which, I can modestly say, is substantial in this town—I'm gonna help you get your job back. Are ya interested?"

"Sure, I'm interested. I just want to know what price I have to pay."

"No price. I'll point you to the truth. Just print it."

"That sounds like an offer of a free lunch, and we all know there is no such thing," said Samuel.

"I have my own reasons for giving you information," he said. "And everything I tell you comes with no strings attached, other than you didn't get the leads from me. Understood?"

Samuel thought for a moment, quickly realizing he didn't have any bargaining power and thus had nothing to lose. "Okay. Where do we go from here?"

"Meet me in my office tomorrow after hours."

"Why don't you meet in my office?" said Melba. "That way no one will see the two of you together."

"Good idea," said Abernathy.

"Can I bring Lieutenant Bernardi, a SFPD homicide detective, with me?"

Abernathy smiled, though Samuel wasn't sure why. "You can bring anybody you want to. Just be sure they'll keep their mouths shut about your source."

"It's a deal," said Samuel, once again shaking the man's rough, calloused hand.

4

Chinatown Has Its Own Woes

As SAMUEL WAS NEGOTIATING with Jim Abernathy, a young girl Samuel had nicknamed Buck Teeth left a message for him at Camelot to contact her at Mr. Song's Many Chinese Herbs shop. Her uncle Mr. Song (whom Samuel privately referred to as the Albino because of his alabaster complexion and pink-rimmed eyes) wished to consult with him on a very important matter. Whenever Mr. Song summoned him, Samuel would drop whatever he was doing and hustle over to the Chinatown herb shop.

When he arrived at the Pacific Avenue address, the tinkling bell above the door announcing his arrival to the dim interior, he looked up to see the familiar garlands of dried herbs hanging from the ceiling. Dozens of terracotta containers were stacked on shelves along two walls that reached from the floor to the eighteen-foot ceiling. Additional floor-to-ceiling shelves along the east wall held even larger jars. Each had an iron top secured by two padlocks, one that could be unlocked by the client, the other by Mr. Song. Samuel knew that Mr. Song's wealthy clients, who didn't trust traditional banks but who also didn't want to hide their life savings beneath their mattresses, kept their money and other valuables in the jars. Bundles of dried herbs hung from the ceiling here as well, emanating pungent and competing aromas.

Looking beyond the black-lacquered counter, whose front panels were painted with traditional Chinese scenes, Samuel saw hundreds of small boxes stacked to the ceiling. Each had a latch secured with a single padlock, and all were numbered with Chinese characters. From his past dealings with Mr. Song, Samuel knew that this was where clients of lesser means kept their savings. A ladder, used to access the jars on the top shelves, leaned against the boxes at one end of the room.

Mr. Song and his niece came out from behind a beaded curtain. Embroidered songbirds decorated the front of Mr. Song's blue Chinese silk jacket. He hadn't changed much since Samuel had last seen him and, as always, wore a skull-cap and thick glasses that magnified his pink-rimmed eyes. Buck Teeth, whose real name was Melody, greeted Samuel. Although she had grown a couple of inches since he last saw her, she was dressed in her usual Gordon plaid skirt, the hem reaching just below her knees, and a starched white blouse with a pagoda emblem on the left pocket.

"Still at the Chinese Baptist School?" asked Samuel as he greeted her.

"Yes, I have one more year to go," said Buck Teeth, smiling and showing the protruding choppers that earned her the nickname. "Thank you for coming, Mr. Hamilton. Mr. Song has a problem and he would like to ask your help. He would like to invite you to have a cup of tea with him. Do you have time?"

"Of course. You tell Mr. Song that I will do everything in my power to help him."

Buck Teeth translated for Mr. Song and then motioned for Samuel to follow her and her uncle through the beaded curtain into the back of the shop, where Samuel found himself in the sitting room where Mr. Song had once hypnotized him to help him stop smoking. After they sat down, Mr. Song stroked his wispy white mustache and goatee and directed a question to his niece. "Mr. Song asks if you are still not smoking?" she said.

"Tell him, for the most part, yes. I had a slip-up a few days ago, but I'm back on track now."

"He says that is good because smoking is not good for you. He also wants to know if Melba quit."

"No, but tell him if that's the only failure he's had in his hypnosis career, he's doing fine." When Buck Teeth finished translating, Mr. Song smiled faintly.

"Have a seat, Mr. Hamilton," said Buck Teeth. "The tea will be here any moment. How do you take it?"

"With sugar, please."

Buck Teeth motioned and an elderly Chinese woman came in through the partially opened door at the back of the sitting room with a tray that contained a teapot, three porcelain cups and cream and sugar containers. She set it down on a table and poured cups for all three. Samuel added a teaspoon of sugar to his and slowly stirred it.

"Mr. Song needs your help, Mr. Hamilton," said Buck Teeth. "Five people in Chinatown have died from mysterious causes in the last week. The health department has reported on their death certificates that they died of natural causes because they were all over seventy. They were not treated at any hospital, and a Chinese doctor was with them when they expired, so no autopsies were performed."

"Were any of them cremated?" asked Samuel.

"All of them. They were Buddhists."

"That's going to make it tough to find out what killed them," said Samuel.

"All of the families have contacted Mr. Song because they think there was foul play," Buck Teeth explained. "They suspect they were poisoned."

"Will they allow us to bring in the police department so

we can test things in their homes?"

"Mr. Song has promised that he will help them. If he tells them that the police are necessary, they will cooperate. As you know, without his guidance, none of this would be possible."

"Yes, I understand that part very well. Are you worried that more people will die from whatever is out there?"

"Yes, Mr. Song thinks it's some kind of a madman on a poison rampage."

"If there's another death and he learns of it quickly, can he convince the family members not to have their loved one cremated?"

"Of course," she answered.

"I'm going to have to bring Lieutenant Bernardi into this. Mr. Song understands that, doesn't he?" Samuel looked at Buck Teeth sympathetically, knowing that he was asking a lot given the distrust the Chinatown community felt for the local authorities. "Without the police and some means of preserving the chain of evidence, we won't have the kind of proof we need to catch the bad guys."

Buck Teeth nodded and bit her lower lip. "He asked me to call you because he knows that you have the wisdom and the kind of connections needed to stop the deaths, and to catch whoever is responsible."

"You understand that I don't have the power to publicize what's going on, since I don't have a job right now."

"Mr. Song knows this and he tells you not to worry. He says that situation won't last long. You are too smart and too good a reporter. That's why he wants you on his team." She smiled, trying not to laugh. "He also thought you'd have a little extra time on your hands now."

Pride and gratitude welled up in Samuel's chest. "Thank him for his confidence in me."

Buck Teeth communicated Samuel's thanks to Mr. Song. The old man smiled faintly in acknowledgment.

"Can I call Bernardi now and set up a meeting for all of us to discuss this problem?"

"It's better if we arrange for the lieutenant and that magic technician who follows him around to go to the home of each of the dead people and ask questions and gather what they think is important evidence," said Buck Teeth.

"Did you figure that out all by yourself?"

"I figured it out from reading your crime stories. And also from watching Charlie Chan movies."

Samuel laughed heartily. "You like Charlie Chan movies? I love them, too. I can't wait until they come out on late night TV. It seems we have a common hero besides Mr. Song."

"Mr. Song is like Judge Dee," said Buck Teeth.

"You mean the Magistrate that Robert Van Gulik wrote about?"

"The same," she answered.

"You know, all those mysteries were written in English, even though the author was Dutch."

"I know his story and Judge Dee's, too," she crowed. "And I've read all seventeen of his mysteries."

"You're a smart cookie. First in your class, I bet?"

"How did you know that?" she asked.

"Very few teenagers are as up-to-date as you are," said Samuel. "That takes brains. Let's see if we can make Charlie Chan's and Judge Dee's principles come to life and help us catch the bad guys." Thinking of the famous judge and the detective, Samuel wondered if there was any possibility that Mr. Song and his niece could channel themselves into the characters. He shook his head. *Let's keep it real*, he said to himself.

* * *

The next day, Samuel, Benardi and Philip Macintosh, the SFPD evidence technician, met Mr. Song and his niece at the

Chinatown shop. From there, they proceeded to the homes of the five families that had unexpectedly lost an elderly family member during the previous week. Their mission was to gather evidence and try to determine if there was a common cause behind the deaths.

While in the process of their investigation, they got a lucky break. Someone called Bernardi to notify him that there had been another unexpected and suspicious death in Chinatown, and gave him the address. The entire group, except for Mr. Song, who remained with the family, stopped what they were doing and rushed off.

The address given was a rickety building next to the Rickshaw bar. Bernardi negotiated his Ford Victoria up Washington Street and parked near the narrow entrance to Ross Alley. The group walked the few yards to the apartment building, where Mr. and Mrs. Chu Chang lived with their family. After climbing three shabby flights of stairs, they knocked at the door of the number they'd been given. Mrs. Chang, a black-clad petite woman with coal black hair and only one front tooth, opened the door and greeted them, her face streaked with tears. The aroma of stale tobacco and rancid cooking oil emanating from the apartment was overwhelming.

Mrs. Chang, two preadolescent children glued to her side, wiped tears from her eyes as she talked to Buck Teeth. She explained that Mr. Chang was down the street, working in a fortune cookie factory, and would be home shortly.

"She says her mother, Mrs. Chow, died suddenly an hour ago," Buck Teeth translated. "She just stopped talking and keeled over."

"Did she have any health problems?" asked Bernardi.

Buck Teeth conferred with Mrs. Chang. "She says no, but you have to understand she was eighty-two years old, so she wasn't a spring chicken."

"May we see her?" asked Bernardi.

At that moment, Mr. Chang, who was only a couple inches taller than his wife, walked in. His blue overalls were speckled with dried dough. He embraced his wife and two children and they followed him into the bedroom, where the family gathered around the pallid corpse of Mrs. Chow.

The guests waited quietly in the dark living room, which was furnished with a worn sofa, two chairs, a large Philco radio receiver and a small RCA television set with protruding rabbit ears. In the corner was an alabaster statute of Buddha.

After a few minutes the family exited their sleeping quarters. Mrs. Chang nodded to her husband and he parted the blue curtain to the bedroom.

"The whole family sleeps in the same room?" said Samuel.

"Of course, this is Chinatown," said Buck Teeth.

"It's a good thing we got here fast," said Samuel. "From the looks of it, they're Buddhists."

"Yes, they were aware of Mr. Song's instructions and called me," said Buck Teeth.

The body of a shriveled woman lay face up on the bed. She looked her age, and her pale face was contorted, as if she had died in pain. She was dressed in a nightgown and her body was partially covered with a plain blanket. Mr. Chang and the children stood grim-faced behind the crowd of officials, staring at the body.

Bernardi whispered to Mac, "Better get the medical examiner up here, right away." He asked Buck Teeth if the family had a phone.

She relayed the message and then pointed to one on the kitchen table. Mac dialed and spoke to someone in the medical examiner's office. When he hung up, he motioned to Buck Teeth. "Can they show us what she last ate? Also, ask them if they ate the same things she did."

Because the apartment was so small, the investigative

crew had to coordinate its movements carefully. Buck Teeth conferred with Mrs. Chang, who directed her to the kitchen. A wok on the two-burner gas stove still held some wilted vegetables. After photographing the scene, Mac gathered the contents of the wok in one of his evidence boxes. "What are all those empty bottles in the kitchen?" he asked.

"They contained mineral water," said Buck Teeth.

"Did everyone in the family drink from them?" he asked.

"No, just the grandmother," answered Buck Teeth. "She didn't like the taste of the tap water, so they humored her. It's an age thing, you know."

Mac put on rubber gloves and placed the three-quart bottles in his evidence box. He then opened the small refrigerator, where he found a variety of vegetables. With the help of Buck Teeth and Mrs. Chang, he labeled them and put them in his box.

"Where do they keep the rice?" he asked. After questioning the children, Buck Teeth pointed to a drawer beneath the stove. Mac opened it and found a five-pound sack.

"What do they use for cooking oil?" he inquired. Buck Teeth conferred with the family once again and then disappeared into the bedroom. A few moments later she returned with a half-full gallon of cooking oil. "They have to keep it in the bedroom because there isn't enough room in the kitchen for everything," she said.

"Do they have any meat?" he asked.

Buck Teeth relayed the question. "Only on Chinese holidays," she said. "The daily meal is vegetables and rice, with tea for the family and mineral water for the grandmother."

"What kind of tea?"

"The tea is right above the stove. They heat tap water to make it."

Mac grabbed the tin of tea. "Sorry, I have to take this to the lab and test it."

When Barney McLeod, the medical examiner, showed up with two men and a gurney, Bernardi moved the family into the living room to make room for the additional team.

"What have we here?" asked Turtle Face.

"An elderly woman died suddenly," answered the Lieutenant.

"And you think that's homicide?"

"I didn't say that," answered Bernardi. "We're following a request from a concerned family, so we investigate. That's all. There have been a series of strange deaths here in Chinatown, and this seems like one of them. We need an autopsy."

"I can accommodate you on that. But frankly, on the face of it, it doesn't seem like you have much. How old was she, and what are you looking for?"

"She was eighty-two," said Bernardi. "But let's see if any poison shows up in her system."

"Okay, boys," said Barney. "Let's take the old gal." They moved the gurney through the curtain leading into the small bedroom, loaded the body and prepared to leave. "You fellows are hanging out in a pretty fancy neighborhood. The Rickshaw bar and Sammy's barbershop are right down the alleyway. Those are two places frequented by the rich and famous."

"This apartment is not included," said Samuel. "It's where the meek live. Those who will inherit the earth."

Turtle Face laughed. "Yeah, that's what I like about this country. The rich and the poor rub elbows and toil together side by side."

"Looks like these folks are lagging pretty far behind," said Samuel.

"All the more reason to try and do something for them," said Buck Teeth.

5

Struggling to Make the System Work

THE MEDICAL EXAMINER RULED the death of Carlos Sanchez a homicide so Samuel spent a lot of time with Bernardi and the D.A., going over the evidence that Bernardi's team had collected at Conklin Chemical. The D.A. had filed an information against Conklin for voluntary manslaughter, and the case was now going before a Municipal Court judge for a preliminary hearing. If the People prevailed he would be held over to the Superior Court and tried for the felony of manslaughter.

Neither the prosecution team nor the police could get a lead on the whereabouts of Sambaguita Poliscarpio, the missing witness, even though there had been an all-points bulletin out on him since he disappeared into the mysterious ambulance at San Francisco General Hospital, and they couldn't postpone the hearing because anyone accused of a crime had the absolute right to be tried within a specified period of time. Conklin's attorneys would not waive that right, even though doing so was a common practice of the defense bar.

The telephone records that were subpoenaed from the phone company showed that the lengthy telephone call Conklin had made on the day of Carlos Sanchez's death was to a registered private investigator named Richard Speckenworth in Green Bay, Wisconsin. His records, in turn, were not accessible based on privilege and lack of jurisdiction by local law enforcement. Mr. Speckenworth was now in San Francisco, working with Conklin's lawyers, which meant that the attorney-client privilege and work product rule protected him from being effectively interrogated by the police or the D.A.

* * *

The day of Conklin's hearing arrived. The case had been assigned to Judge Hiram Peterson. He was an up-and-coming jurist who had been appointed to the Municipal Court by former Governor Goodie Knight, a Republican, in 1959. He had recently been elevated to the Superior Court by Knight's successor, Edmund J. Brown, a Democrat, so this was his last case in the inferior court. Not only was his future as a jurist now secure, he'd also made a name for himself with both political parties as an aggressive prosecutor.

"What do we know about this guy?" Bernardi asked Samuel.

"He graduated from Harvard Law School *cum laude* and then worked for the U.S. Attorney's office in San Francisco for a few years as a prosecutor, alongside our own D.A. and my college buddy, Charles Perkins."

"Oh, shit. A prick off the old cock?" Bernardi laughed sarcastically.

"Who's the prick?" responded Samuel, also laughing.

"Since we're speaking privately, you figure it out."

"Perkins says he's quick-witted and a suave conversationalist. He also said that his objective isn't to climb the judicial ladder, it's political. He decided that a judgeship was the quickest way to get where he was going, either the governorship or a seat in the U.S. Senate. The way he got such a quick promotion is that he ingratiated himself to powerful people he thought could help him."

"The D.A. says he's tough on crime," said Bernardi. "That's who he wants to hear this case. I personally have my doubts."

"Yeah. He sounds like a kiss-ass."

"We'll see. I asked the D.A. to challenge him, but he said it wasn't good politics."

The judge, dressed in his black robe, entered the courtroom through the back door and climbed the few steps to the dais. He was right out of central casting, with a strong jaw and a full head of steel-gray hair. Once seated, he nodded to the clerk.

The clerk called the case: "People of the State of California versus Chad Conklin."

The young deputy District Attorney stood, gave his name and announced that the People were ready.

The well-tailored attorney standing next to him spoke next. "James Morrison of Pillsbury, Madison and Sutro ready for the defendant, Chad Conklin."

"Your Honor, we'd like to ask for a continuance, as there is a missing witness," said the deputy District Attorney.

"We object to any continuance," the defense attorney countered. "The defendant has not waived time."

"Submitted?"

Both attorneys answered yes.

"The motion is denied. Do the People have a time estimate?"

"The People estimate two days."

"We estimate ten minutes."

The Assistant D.A. shrugged his shoulders knowingly. He'd heard that one before.

"Very well, call your first witness."

"Before we get started, your honor, we request that all potential witnesses be excluded from the court room," said the defense attorney.

"Any objection, Counsel?" the judge asked.

"No, your honor."

"Very well, that's the ruling of the court. All potential witnesses are excluded from the court until it's time for their testimony."

The deputy called Roberto Sanchez, the cousin of the dead worker. After his near-brush with death, Sanchez was now fifteen pounds lighter, which gave him a birdlike appearance, and he spoke with a hoarse voice, his breath labored.

The Assistant D.A. asked Sanchez to describe, in detail, the steps he and his cousin took to get into the tank and what happened afterward. The deputy also asked him to describe the equipment they were given. Sanchez's testimony was interrupted several times when he had trouble breathing, and at one point he broke down sobbing as he described the plight of his stricken cousin.

Everyone in the courtroom waited respectfully for Sanchez to compose himself.

"Had you ever used an oxygen mask at Conklin Chemical before the date of the accident?"

"No, sir."

"Had you ever seen one before?"

"Yes, sir."

"When?"

"One time the health department come to inspect the plant for safety," said Sanchez, his testimony slowed by wheezing and coughing. "They knowed they was coming so the bookkeeper gave us masks to carry around, and we was tol' to say that we had them with us all the time, if someone ask us."

"Was that true?"

"No, sir. When the man from the health department left, the bookkeeper took them back. I never saw one again until the day of the accident."

The deputy then asked Sanchez to describe his brother's

last minutes of life in the tank and what he remembered about being rescued.

The defense attorney asked only one question on cross-examination. "Do you think that Mr. Conklin wished you or your cousin intentional physical harm?"

The deputy jumped to his feet. "Objection! It's irrelevant what he thought Mr. Conklin wished him."

"Overruled, he may answer."

"No, sir. He was a good boss. He paid well."

Bernardi was the next witness and took the stand in the afternoon. He explained to the judge how he had examined all the oxygen masks that the workers had used, along with the untouched ones in the tool room. The use-by dates on all the masks had expired, he said, adding that it wasn't safe for any of them to be used in a confined space without proper ventilation. Bernardi stated that there was simply no assurance that the masks would provide emergency oxygen to the workers when needed.

He then testified how he had tried to find the missing witness, only to discover that he'd disappeared.

The defense attorney took over. "Lieutenant Bernardi, do you and/or the SFPD have a vendetta against Mr. Conklin?"

"No, sir."

"Are you claiming that Mr. Conklin is responsible for the disappearance of the witness, Mr. Poliscarpio?"

"It looks suspicious, don't you think?"

"Move to strike!" yelled the defense counsel. "It calls for speculation and innuendo."

"Sustained," said the judge, slamming down his gavel. "Stick to the facts, Lieutenant Bernardi."

"No further questions," said the defense attorney.

Philip Macintosh, Bernardi's tech, was up next, and used his time on the stand to establish that none of the five masks had any oxygen in them when they were tested.

When the defense attorney took over, he in turn attempted to establish that Macintosh's examination took place long after the accident.

"No, sir," Macintosh countered. "They were tested right after it happened. The ambulance carrying the injured workers had just left and the medical examiner was on-site collecting the decedent."

The deputy then called Marcel Fabreceaux, Samuel's photographer. He had him identify the photos he took of Conklin wiping the dead man's face with a cloth.

The defense lawyer began his line of questioning. "Did you have any knowledge of the man being dead when you took the photo?"

"No sir, I just shot the photo."

"And you never got near enough to actually see the man himself, did you?"

"What you see in the photo is the closest I got."

The Deputy D.A. resumed his questioning. "By the time you took this photo, had the other two injured parties already been removed by ambulance?"

"Yes, sir."

The next morning, the Deputy D.A. called Milford Jackson, the ambulance driver, who testified that he picked up the injured workers, Roberto Sanchez and Sambaguita Poliscarpio, and took them to San Francisco General Hospital in his ambulance.

"Was there another victim at the scene?"

"Yes, sir. We were going to take him, too, but he was dead."

"Objection!" called out the defense attorney. "No foundation. There is no testimony that this man is a doctor or even knows what a dead man looks or acts like."

"Lay the foundation," said the judge.

"Very well, Your Honor," said the deputy. "How long have

you been an ambulance driver, Mr. Jackson?"

"Twelve years."

"Have you attended to dead people during that time?"

"Yes, sir.

"How did you know they were dead?"

"Lots of different reasons. Sometimes they had a big hole in their head or their chest, but most of the time when there ain't no trauma, they just ain't breathing, there's no pulse and their eyes are wide open."

"Over the years, how many dead persons have you encountered in your work?"

"I'd say around a hundred."

"Ever wrong about your opinion that a person was in fact dead?"

"No, sir."

"Explain to the court in what condition you found Mr. Carlos Sanchez."

"He was lying face-up on the ground. He was wet—I assumed from being hosed down—but he still had a lot of brown sludge all over him, including on his face. He had no pulse; he wasn't breathing and his eyes were wide open."

"Did you have a conversation with anyone at that time?"

"Yes, sir."

"With whom?"

"That man, sitting right over there," he said, pointing to Conklin.

"What did you tell him?"

"That the man was dead and I was radioing in for them to call the medical examiner."

"Did he say anything to you?"

"He gave me an angry stare and turned towards the man lying on the ground."

"Objection!" shouted the defense attorney. "Move to strike. What's an angry stare? Calls for speculation."

"Overruled."

"Did you radio in for someone to call the medical examiner?"

"Yes, sir. The dispatcher."

"When you got to the hospital with the injured workmen, what happened to Mr. Poliscarpio?"

"You mean the Filipino?"

"Is that how you describe him?"

"Yes, sir."

"Well, what happened to him?"

"There was a white ambulance waiting there and it took him away."

"Do you know where it took him?"

"No, sir. They didn't say nothing 'cept that they had orders to take him. The man signed for him, then he and his helper loaded him in their ambulance and took off."

"Can you describe them?"

"Two white guys. A little taller than me and both heavier."

"Ever see either of them before?"

"No, sir."

"Or again?"

"No, sir."

"Thank you, Mr. Jackson."

The defense attorney stood up and walked slowly over to the witness, coming to a stop directly in front of him, his face so close the ambulance driver could feel the lawyer's breath on his cheek. "You're not a doctor are you, Mr. Jackson?" he asked in a low, measured tone.

"No, sir."

"And you're not a paramedic either, are you?" His voice was practically a whisper.

"No, sir."

The defense attorney raised his voice. "When the two

white men in the white ambulance took the Filipino away, they never said that they were taking orders from Mr. Conklin, did they?"

"No, sir."

"In fact, they never said who sent them."

"They said that Conklin Chemical sent them."

"Nothing further. Move to strike the witness's testimony about Mr. Sanchez being dead, and that Conklin Chemical sent them. No foundation."

"Overruled. Call your next witness, Counsel."

"We have subpoenaed Mr. James Hooker for this afternoon," said the deputy attorney. "Can we take the noon recess?"

"Very well. Court's adjourned until 2 p.m."

* * *

"What is your job, Mr. Hooker?"

"I'm the bookkeeper at Conklin Chemical."

"Are you still employed there?"

"Yes, sir."

"Do you know the whereabouts of Mr. Sambaguita Poliscarpio?"

"No, sir."

"Since the date of the accident, have you made any payments for his care or treatment?"

"No, sir."

"Is he still an employee of Conklin Chemical?"

"Yes, sir."

"Are you paying him?"

"I can't pay him if I can't find him."

"Let me show you this photograph. It's marked 'People's Exhibit No. 25.' Is that you kneeling next to Mr. Sanchez?"

"Yes, sir."

"Is that a rag in your hand?"

"Yes, sir."

"Were you cleaning sludge off of Mr. Sanchez's face with it?"

"No, sir. We'd been working on him, trying to revive him and I got the stuff all over my hands."

"Wasn't he already dead as you were kneeling there?"

"I wasn't told that. I was still trying to help Mr. Conklin revive him."

"How was Mr. Conklin trying to revive him?"

"He was cleaning the sludge off of him so he could continue with artificial respiration."

"Is that what he was doing in this photo, 'People's Exhibit No. 26'?"

"Yes, sir. As well as I remember."

"This photo shows him cleaning sludge off the man's face. Is that right?"

"I'm not sure what he was doing in that photo. That was a long time ago."

"After this photo was taken, did you see him give Mr. Sanchez artificial respiration?"

"I'm sorry. I don't remember. That was a long time ago."

"Is Mr. Roberto Sanchez still an employee of Conklin Chemical?"

"Yes, sir. But right now he's on disability. He's supposed to come back to work next week."

"Who pays his disability?"

"Our workers' compensation insurance company."

"Which is?"

"Employer's Insurance Company of Saint Paul."

"After this accident occurred did you call an ambulance company and tell it to pick up Sambaguita Poliscarpio at the San Francisco General Hospital?"

"No, sir."

"Did you hear anyone else at Conklin Chemical call an ambulance company and say those words on the day of the accident?"

"No, sir."

"Thank you. That's all I have."

"I have a couple more questions, said the defense attorney.

"You weren't with Mr. Conklin every second during this time, is that correct?"

"No, sir. It was a madhouse."

"When Mr. Conklin was on the phone, did you overhear any of his conversation?"

"If he was on the phone, I wasn't aware of it."

"That's all I have of this witness for the time being."

"Call your next witness," ordered the judge, putting down his pen and pouring a drink of water from the pitcher on the dais.

"We'll call Samuel Hamilton."

Samuel took the witness stand and was sworn in. He was dressed in his usual khaki sports coat, which was neatly ironed. He had on a clean, pressed madras shirt and shined penny loafers. Samuel was angry that he'd been kept out of the courtroom until now. He wanted to know what was going on all the time.

"Were you a reporter on the day of the accident at Conklin Chemical?"

"Yes, sir."

"And were you present when these two photos, exhibits '25' and '26', were taken?"

"Yes, sir. I told Mr. Fabreceaux, who was my photographer, to take them."

"Why did you want them taken?"

"Because the ambulance driver, Mr. Jackson, told Mr. Conklin and his bookkeeper that Mr. Sanchez was dead, but they still kept cleaning his face with rags. I thought that was strange so I wanted a record of it."

"You had no doubt that Mr. Sanchez was dead?"

"I had no doubt. I heard the ambulance driver say so and also say that he was going to radio in to have them call the medical examiner."

"Were Mr. Conklin and Mr. Hooker there, too?"

"Yes, sir. They were right next to where I was."

"Did you say anything about this to Mr. Conklin?"

"I was going to, but he kicked me and the photographer off his property."

"Had you finished doing your jobs when that happened?"

"Objection, it was Mr. Conklin's private property!" yelled the defense attorney.

"Sustained," said the judge.

"Your Honor, we would like to pursue this line of questioning. It goes to Mr. Conklin's state of mind in trying to conceal evidence."

"I've already ruled, Counsel. Let's move on."

"Very well, I'm finished with this witness."

The defense attorney stood up and stared at Samuel for a full minute before he spoke. "You were fired for telling lies in the paper about Mr. Conklin, weren't you?"

"Objection, it's argumentative," said the deputy.

"Overruled. This is cross-examination."

"Mr. Conklin will have to prove that," said Samuel defiantly. "I didn't tell lies about anyone."

"But you haven't had a job since two days after the accident. Isn't that true?"

"Yes, that's true."

"And you were fired the day after you wrote an article about Mr. Conklin and the accident, isn't that true?"

"I was put on leave without pay, that's true, but not because I told a lie. It was because my employer got a letter from your firm threatening to sue the paper I work for unless it fired me. There's a big difference between what happened and what you're trying to make of it."

"I see. You want to explain it to the judge?"

"Objection, argumentative."

"I withdraw the question. I'm through with this witness."

Samuel sat down with the rest of the onlookers. Since he'd already testified, he was now free to be in the courtroom.

"The People rest," said the deputy.

"The defense rests," said Conklin's attorney. "And we ask that the charges be dismissed. The People have not established probable cause."

"We'll get to that in a moment," said the judge. "Do the People wish to be heard?"

"Yes, Your Honor. We've more than established probable cause. Mr. Conklin was showing off the masks when the health department came around. Either he personally knew they were worthless, or he didn't care enough about the safety of his workers to check and see if they were. Putting them in danger in an enclosed tank without checking is criminal enough to hold him over. That's all it takes. At this stage of the proceedings we don't have to prove anything beyond a reasonable doubt."

"Defense counsel?"

"There is no probable cause. All we have here is an accident. That's not enough to sustain or continue with this charade."

"Is that it, gentlemen?"

Both attorneys nodded their heads.

"Very well. The defendant is free to go. The court finds there is no probable cause that a crime was committed."

Conklin strode arrogantly out the courtroom and put on his dark glasses. He brushed past the reporters huddled outside the door without comment, his lawyer walking a few paces behind carrying two bulging briefcases.

"Did you expect that result?" Samuel asked the Assistant D.A.

"When I heard the judge announce his decision, I felt my mouth fall open. In the two years I've worked as a prosecutor, no defendant has walked away from a preliminary hearing without being charged with something."

"Is that it?" asked Samuel. "Is he going to get away with this?"

"The first thing we have to do is find the witness. If he'll talk and confirm that Conklin sent him away to hide, I'm sure the D.A. will send it to the Grand Jury and ask for an indictment."

"What about double jeopardy?" asked Samuel.

"It won't apply. It's complicated, but I'll explain it to you some time." He looked tired and dejected.

Samuel rushed upstairs to Bernardi's office to tell him the result.

Bernardi frowned. "I'm surprised. We'll have to put our heads together and find that witness, if he's still alive."

"Do you think that Conklin had him bumped off?" asked Samuel.

"From what I've seen so far, I wouldn't put anything past that bastard."

"Remember I told you that Jim Abernathy said he would help me? I think it's time to take him up on his offer. There has to be some trace of Poliscarpio somewhere, and the Assistant D.A. said if we discover his whereabouts and he cooperates, the D.A. can take the case to the Grand Jury and we won't need a preliminary hearing. But what do you think about the judge?"

"I'm not so worried about him. The D.A. wanted to look good and he jumped the gun. I told him we needed the key witness, but he didn't want to wait. So, it's on him."

"Conklin wouldn't waive time," said Samuel. "The D.A. had no choice, he had to have the preliminary hearing. None of this helps me any. Now it looks like the paper was justified in giving me the boot. I could see Conklin puffing up like a blowfish—he thinks he's so powerful. I'm telling you right now, Bruno, he's a lying son of a bitch, and I'm going to prove it."

"I agree, and I'm going to help you," said Bernardi.

6

The Real Cost of Bottled Water

BARNEY MCLEOD SHUFFLED the papers on his desk until he found the report he was looking for. "It was poison, alright," he said to Samuel and Bernardi, who were sitting opposite him. "Enough arsenic in that bottle of mineral water to kill a horse."

"Mr. Song was right," said Samuel. Then, turning to Bernardi, "Where do we go from here?"

"First thing we do is get the State Attorney General to shut down the operation and then force the company to recall all the product it maufactures. We also need to make sure it doesn't destroy any of its product or other material evidence. At the same time, we get our people in there with the health department to find out exactly how this happened and where the arsenic came from. It's already clear to me that it couldn't have come from the Hetch Hetchy water system because it delivers the cleanest water in Northern California."

"You think it's the water?" asked Samuel.

"Hell, yes," said Barney. "My bet is whoever the owner is brought water in from somewhere in the central valley because it was cheap, and bottled it right here in Chinatown."

"I'll call the Attorney General and get him and his staff on board," said Bernardi."

"You think the owner is the one responsible?" asked Samuel.

"I'll bet you ten bucks."

"That's one bet I won't take. I've lost enough on the Forty-Niners."

* * *

At least twenty people, including Samuel, Bernardi, Philip Macintosh, Buck Teeth and Assistant Attorney General Jack Bruschet, were gathered in front of a ramshackle brick building on Trenton Street, in the heart of Chinatown. A dingy yellow sign above the entrance announced the building was home to the Flower Blossom Mineral Water Bottling Company.

Bruschet was tall and had disheveled curly brown hair. He wore a cheap, off-the-rack black suit and scuffed brown shoes. His white shirt was wrinkled and his blue tie spattered with some of last night's dinner—and probably that morning's breakfast as well. In short, he was the perfect image of a dedicated civil servant, down to the strong jaw and humorless expression.

The Assistant Attorney General pounded on the door. When no one answered, he kicked the door open, rushing through with two gun-wielding State Marshals in tow. Buck Teeth and the rest of the entourage followed on his heels. "We demand access to these premises on behalf of the Attorney General of the State of California," Bruschet yelled, waving his sheaf of papers in the air.

At first glance, the cavernous, windowless room appeared deserted, holding nothing more than three massive tanks. The room was hot and the faint smell of almonds hung in the thick air. But as the group's eyes adjusted, they made out three Chinese workmen, one hiding behind each of the tanks. Buck Teeth was the first to see the men, and, realizing how frightened they were, quickly spoke to them in Cantonese.

"These men are not here to harm you," she reassured them. "They are looking for the owner. Do you know where he is?"

The three looked at each other in surprise and then stared blankly at Buck Teeth. One of them finally spoke. "None of us knows who the owner is," he said in Cantonese. "We work for Mr. Huang Wang. He tells us what to do."

"Where is Mr. Wang?" she asked.

"He doesn't come until after noodle time, maybe afternoon," the spokesman said.

"Where do you put the water in the bottles?" she asked.

"In the building next to this one."

"What are these tanks for?"

"This is where the water is boiled."

"Where does the water come from?"

"A big truck brings it twice a week at six in the morning."

"Where does the truck come from?"

They all shrugged their shoulders. "You have to ask Mr. Wang."

"The attorney who is with me says this business is registered to Mr. Min Fu-Hok. Have you ever seen him here?"

There was no answer, so she asked again. The three men shook their heads.

After she had finished relaying the men's answers to the investigators, an impatient Bruschet took over. "Enough of this bullshit!" he barked at the three men cowering behind the tanks, not even waiting for Buck Teeth to translate. "You tell your boss this bottling company is shut down." He took a roll of tape out of his pocket, pulled the cease and desist order out of his sheaf of papers and pasted it on one of the tanks. He then pasted another copy on the outside of the door he had kicked in. "Lieutenant, we need your crime lab to gather samples of the water in these tanks and then confiscate all the bottles that are ready for shipment."

"We can take care of all that for you, Mr. Bruschet," said Bernardi. "But we also need evidence for our case. Remember, this is a homicide investigation as well as a cease and desist proceeding."

"Attorney General Mosk is on your side, Lieutenant. Anything you need that doesn't interfere with our preventing harm to the people of California will be allowed."

"Thank you, Mr. Bruschet. I take that as permission for my people to do their job." Bernardi virtually pushed the attorney out of the way and directed his team to secure the evidence.

"We need to find out where the water came from," said Samuel.

"We will, but our job right now is to stop this maniac from producing or distributing any more bottles of poisoned water."

"Can you find out from these workers if they know of anyone else who works for the company?" Samuel asked Mr. Song's niece, Melody.

"Give me a few minutes. They're scared out of their wits. This man might be a good attorney, but he doesn't know anything about public relations or Chinese customs."

She took the workers over to the corner of the dank room and spoke to them quietly. Bernardi and Mac followed a hose from one of the three water tanks into another building, where the crates of bottled water were stacked floor-to-ceiling next to an old-fashioned bottling machine. A plate with the words "Hamm's Brewery, San Francisco" was affixed to the side of the machine, along with "1934," the year it was manufactured.

"Look at that," said Samuel. "This machine must have been fabricated in response to the repeal of prohibition. Mr. Min had to have picked it up pretty cheap, judging from the rest of this operation."

"Yeah," said Bernardi. "It's put together with electric tape and wire."

"And poisoned water," added Samuel. "Don't you think it's interesting that there's no one around?"

"Would you stick around if someone was kicking down the door of your place of employment?" asked Mac.

"I hope Buck Teeth can fill in the missing pieces," said Samuel. "Bruschet reminds me of Perkins. Two civil servants created out of the same mold."

"Bruschet really is trying to protect the people, though; Perkins is only out for himself," said Bernardi.

The crew confiscated all the cases of water and tested the tanks for toxic chemicals. Mac was astounded by the results. "There is so much arsenic in that water that it's unexplainable," he said. "Could it be that someone was putting it in intentionally?"

"Was there any arsenic in the bottled water?" asked Samuel.

"Plenty, and it's a good thing we stopped this when we did. There is almost double that amount in the water tank. If the average person had a dose from a bottle of it, it could kill him on the spot."

By that time, Buck Teeth had returned to the bottling plant with the three workmen they'd found hidden behind the tanks. "They say there are twelve employees who work here, and they've given me their names," she told them. "We can find them through Mr. Song. Also, they told me that the water comes from the Fort Ross State Park."

"So they know more than they at first let on," said Samuel.

"Yes, but you can't blame them for not talking. They were scared," said Buck Teeth.

"Fort Ross is north of Jenner, on the coast?" asked Bernardi.

"Yes," said Buck Teeth. "The boss sends a tanker truck up there twice a week, and they take it out of the river."

"Has one of them ever gone up there to get water?" asked Samuel.

"Yes, they all have."

"Who chose the spot?"

"Mr. Min. He told them it was free, and that if they were ever stopped, they were to tell the authorities that they were getting the water for irrigation."

"Do any of them write or read English?" asked Bernardi.

"No, but I can get each of them to give a recorded statement in Cantonese," she answered.

"Ask them if they know where we can find Mr. Min," said Samuel. Buck Teeth's question, however, was met with blank stares.

7

Every Parent's Nightmare

JIM ABERNATHY WAS THE JUNK king of the San Francisco Bay Area.

He built an empire after first buying a junkyard in the industrial section of West Oakland and then building the business up to become the leading U.S. exporter of used steel to the Far East. After his wife's death, however, he became intent on giving his three children—Margaret, the eldest, James Jr., and Grace—all the resources he'd lacked back in Ireland and as a new immigrant to America.

Since Grace never knew her mother, who died giving birth to her, her father devoted most of his free time to ensuring that she would excel both in her studies and her social life. He paid for expensive dance and singing lessons and made sure she was given extra tutoring in academics. As a result, Grace, an excellent student, was easily accepted at the University of California in Berkeley. Although she wasn't the best-looking coed at Berkeley, she was attractive enough and, more important, she was wealthy. She joined the prestigious Kappa Kappa Gamma sorority and was wooed both by wealthy young men eager to increase their social and financial standing in the upper echelons of San Francisco society and by up-and-comers like Chad Conklin—captain of the football team and a Big

Man on Campus—who coveted the entrée she afforded to the city's inner circles of power.

Conklin won the contest and he and Grace were married upon their graduation in June of 1959. Their wedding was one of San Francisco's biggest social events of the year, and soon after Conklin left to complete his two-year Reserve Officers' Training Corps military obligation.

While Chad was in the Navy, Grace metamorphosed into a leading socialite and fashion icon. She still had the driving ambition to be on top that had gotten her through Berkeley as a member of the ruling class.

After Conklin came back from his naval assignment he focused his energies on building his empire at Conklin Chemical, and it didn't take long before the business was in the black. With ever-increasing profits in hand, he made a sizeable down payment on a house in Piedmont, a wealthy city in the East Bay, which was surrounded by the much larger, and less affluent, city of Oakland. Both the house and the community met his requirement for the appearance of success. Because of his athletic connections he was welcomed into the exclusive Claremont Country Club, where he played golf with business connections and people he was trying to impress. He also encouraged Sambaguita Poliscarpio, his Filipino foreman, to learn how to play at the municipal course—he couldn't take him to his own club, where non-whites were unwelcome—as it was a useful game to play with business contacts visiting from the Far East.

At first, Grace thought she was happy. Conklin was a good provider, he didn't drink and he was going places. He also had the very deep pockets she was used to. She applied her many talents to the home front, turning their garden into a showplace and lining the walls of the house with expensive art. But she soon realized that Conklin wasn't making himself available to her emotionally. When she summoned the courage to confront him, asking him to spend more time at home, he brushed her off, saying that he was busy at work.

Even though her unhappiness was growing, Grace accepted the work excuse for a while, but finally came to the grim understanding that her husband had no interest in her. He was either at the club playing golf with business associates or was huddled at the office with Sambaguita, figuring out how to squeeze more money out of his chemical business.

She'd expected a storybook life, complete with the college hero and a picture-perfect Donna Reed family. Though they did look handsome together at social events—Grace on Chad's arm, her smile gracious and infectious—people would have been shocked to learn of the true emptiness of their relationship.

One evening, she again pleaded again with Chad over a candle-lit dinner she had prepared specially. "We just can't go on like this," she complained, twisting her napkin in her lap, her brow furrowed with anguish. "I thought you wanted a real marriage. You don't even look at me anymore, and you're never around. I need sex more than once a month and I want children."

"There are two sides to every story," he answered with exaggerated disdain. "I have observed you flitting around this house, the garden, the country club and wherever else. You don't lift a finger to make my life more comfortable or complete. You just sit on your ass and let other people do it or it doesn't get done. What's more, you spend money like a country at war."

"It's you who wants me to look nice and wear expensive clothes and be seen at the club and with the right people!" she screamed, the pain of her husband's rejection stabbing her heart.

"Goddamn it," he swore, his face turning red. "You can't get by just by being a fashion plate and trying to look like a porcelain doll." He glared at her and pointed his finger menacingly. "I thought you were going to be an asset to my career, not just another cross I had to bear. You complain and whine all the time, while I do all the work!"

She stood and slapped him in the face, then bolted from the dinner table. Sobbing, she ran to the guestroom and locked the door behind her. Chad slept alone that night and for several nights thereafter. Soon they had separate bedrooms. The die had been cast for the remainder of their relationship: it was for appearances only. If she wanted more, she would have to find it elsewhere.

The truth of the matter was that Conklin had no real interest in Grace beyond using her to get ahead financially and as a way to make powerful connections in San Francisco. In the end, it came down to the fact that he was focused on using any and all means to become a successful businessman and she was lonely and depressed. This marriage that wasn't meant to be was coming apart—a result that Jim Abernathy had predicted early in their relationship.

* * *

A few months after their dinner confrontation, Grace walked to a bus stop in San Francisco and waited for a bus to take her back to Piedmont. As she sat down on the weathered bench, she put her head down in her folded arms and sobbed. "How could I have done this to myself?"

When she looked up, she saw an old, shabbily dressed wino, a giant wilted daisy in his hands, watching her from a short distance away. There was no one else around. He raised the flower towards her. She wiped her tear-stained face and smiled wanly, slowly shaking her head. He continued to approach, still extending the wilted daisy. When he reached the bench his attitude shifted and he darted behind her, taking a cord out of his coat pocket and wrapping it around her neck.

She struggled and kicked and tried to yell, but her assailant tightened the cord, twisting it with a baton, and she could only manage gurgling sounds. Her flailing lasted only a short time before she slumped, lifeless, onto the bench. As the shadows of early evening closed in on the deserted street, the man dragged her body behind the bench where it couldn't be seen.

Shortly afterward, the bus that Grace had been waiting for stopped in front of the empty bench. Its front doors opened and two passengers exited, each walking off in a different direction.

* * *

Samuel was at Bernardi's office the next morning at ten, having heard about Grace Conklin's murder from his police band sources earlier in the day. He saluted the detective with a wave and got straight to business. "The death of this young woman is unbelievable," said Samuel. "Are there any clues as to who did it?"

"Not enough to point the finger anywhere," said Bernardi. "But we're looking at everything that was found at the scene. It's a bus stop, so who the hell knows how many people a day pass by there."

"Barney told Conklin that she was dead, but I doubt that he's said anything to Jim Abernathy," said Samuel. "We should be the ones to break it to him."

"Good thinking, Samuel. Poor man is going to take it pretty hard."

Later that afternoon, Samuel went with Bernardi to Abernathy's office next to the port in West Oakland. It was where the Junk King stored all the flattened cars and other steel that was subsequently loaded onto vessels and shipped to the Far East. That was the business that made Mr. Abernathy a very wealthy man.

As they rolled up to the entrance gate, an armed security

guard stopped them. His uniform was black and he had a patch on his left sleeve, just below the shoulder, that read Sheffield Security. "State your business," he growled.

"I'm here on police business," said Bernardi. "Tell Mr. Abernathy that Lieutenant Bernardi of the San Francisco Police Department wishes to speak with him."

The guard flinched when he heard the word "police," then squinted as he scrutinized Bernardi's faded brown suit and short haircut.

Samuel thought that the guard probably didn't believe Bernardi was a cop.

"I need some identification, sir."

Bernardi whipped out his shield and flashed it at the guard.

"Sorry, sir. Can't be too careful in this neighborhood," said the guard, smiling for the first time. He walked the few steps to the gate and unlocked it, swinging it open. "It's the building down by the waterfront, next to the pier." He motioned towards the bay.

Bernardi parked next to a beige, single story building and he and Samuel got out. They climbed the steps onto the wooden porch and entered the structure through a plain door, where they found a receptionist sitting at an expensive rosewood desk. She wore glasses and her hair was pulled back in a bun. There was a telephone switchboard to her right and a Teletype machine behind her. On her left, a stock market ticker spit out market numbers minute to minute. Behind her desk was a large Irish flag, encased in glass. A plaque noted that the flag had been signed by Michael Collins.

"Who's Michael Collins?" asked Bernardi.

"He was an Irish patriot in charge of the Irish army," said Samuel. "Rumor has it he was murdered by his own men in 1922."

"How did you know that?" asked Bernardi.

"I read stuff."

The secretary looked at the two men curiously.

They introduced themselves and Bernardi showed his credentials. She plugged a jack into the switchboard and announced the visitors. Within seconds, Abernathy opened a door at the far end of the office.

He was dressed in a black pinstriped suit, a stiff white shirt and an expensive red tie. "Come in, Lieutenant, and hello, Mr. Hamilton. I've been looking forward to our meeting. Is that why you're here? Did you think you needed police protection to discuss that conniving bastard Chad Conklin with me?" He smiled.

"Unfortunately, that's not why we're here," said Samuel. "The lieutenant will explain."

Abernathy's smile turned into a frown. "Is this official police business?" he asked, looking first at Bernardi and then Samuel.

"Let's go into your office, if you don't mind," said Bernardi.

Once inside his elegant and spacious office, Abernathy sank into his overstuffed brown leather chair, folded his hands and placed them in his lap. On the blotter was a cup of steaming coffee in a fancy porcelain cup. Samuel was surprised at the intensity with which Abernathy stared at them; he looked like a crouching tiger waiting to attack.

"All right, goddamn it, let's have it," he barked.

"We come with bad news," said Samuel sadly.

Abernathy jerked. "What bad news?" He squinted at the reporter.

"Your daughter Grace has been murdered," said Bernardi.

There was silence in the room. Abernathy's face slowly turned crimson. His eyes exhibited a savage, haunted look that Samuel had never seen before in his life. His wiry frame bolted from the overstuffed chair, as if he had been shot out of a cannon. He grabbed the cup of coffee and hurled it against the wall to the right of where Samuel and Bernardi were standing, splattering the desk, the floor and the wall with coffee and pieces of porcelain.

"That motherfucker Conklin killed her. I want his ass, Lieutenant. I know it was him," he ranted. As he sat back down, his rage dissipated. His face paled, and he folded in on himself, appearing suddenly small and vulnerable. Abernathy tried to talk, but no words came out. "When…?" he finally managed to get out, his voice a ragged whisper.

"Last night at a bus stop in San Francisco, near the Bay Bridge."

"What kind of a depraved bastard would do a thing like that? Do you have any proof it was Conklin?"

Bernardi shook his head. "Right now we don't know who did it. Your daughter was found behind a bench at a bus stop. She had been strangled. The medical examiner has notified her husband, but Samuel and I thought that we should tell you instead of him, since, from what I understand, you have a pretty difficult relationship with him."

"Difficult isn't the word for it, Lieutenant. I'm sitting here thinking that son of a bitch killed her or had her killed so he could get his hands on her money. I'm sure Samuel told you they had a shitty relationship." He put his head down on his desk and began to sob. His wails were loud and deep.

His secretary rushed into the room and cried, "What on earth has happened?"

Abernathy lifted his head from his desk. Between sobs, he cried, "Someone killed my baby girl! Someone killed my baby girl!" He put his head back down on his desk, his body once again wracked with convulsive sobs.

The secretary began to cry and moved to approach Abernathy, but Bernardi motioned for her to stop. "You have to let him get it out of his system. Otherwise, he won't be able to function."

"Should I call his doctor?" she asked in a shaky voice.

"Not a bad idea," said Samuel, and Bernardi nodded his approval.

She rushed out of the room, closing the door behind her.

"Is there anything we can do for you, Mr. Abernathy?" asked Bernardi.

The man straightened up in his chair. "Not right now, Lieutenant. I need to get home to my other children. I can't possibly tell them something like this over the telephone."

He stood up, pulled down on the sides of his suit jacket and adjusted his tie. "If you need that job, Mr. Hamilton, it's still available," he said, his voice cracking. "After we've laid my baby to rest, let's talk."

He shook hands with both men and they left the office together, Abernathy calling over his shoulder to his secretary. "Tell the doctor to come to my house, but don't tell him why. My kids are going to need a lot of help to get through this. Grace was the baby of the family."

* * *

One of the biggest funerals in San Francisco history was held at Old Saint Mary's Cathedral on California Street, at the corner of Grant Avenue in the heart of Chinatown. Over three thousand people from every walk of life came to say goodbye to Grace Abernathy. They crowded the sidewalks and the streets outside the red brick structure, which had housed the church since the middle of the nineteenth century.

The Archbishop of the diocese gave the eulogy. Samuel sat inside the church with Melba and her daughter Blanche, while Bernardi sat with his girlfriend Marisol. The Abernathy family occupied the first pew on one side of the first aisle, with Conklin sitting alone in the first pew of the other.

The mass was inspiring, and towards the end of it, a small chorus from the San Francisco Symphony came through the side door, surrounded the flower-draped coffin and, accompanied by the church organist, sang Lacrimosa from Mozart's Requiem Mass and Ave Maria. When it was over, the sixteen pallbearers, including Jim Abernathy and his son, James Jr., moved to the coffin and walked it slowly down the aisle to the waiting hearse.

Chad Conklin was not among them.

* * *

After Grace was laid to rest in the family crypt next to her mother at the Holy Cross Catholic Cemetery in Colma, just south of the city, the mourners descended on Camelot. The bar filled with more than two hundred mourners, all wanting to drink Irish whiskey. Melba was prepared. She'd hired five extra bartenders and a bagpiper and put up a sign that drinks were on the house. Relieved of her usual bartending duties, Blanche was free to mingle with the crowd. Grace's family and friends gathered in groups, tearfully remembering her during her formative years, and the crowd periodically burst into Irish laments and lullabies. The principal of the Sacred Heart School, from which Grace had graduated with straight A's, eulogized her in a lengthy, tear-filled speech, during the course of which no one so much as whispered.

Samuel and Blanche stayed until dark and then snuck away to his apartment.

8

Too Many Dead People

IT WAS AFTER MIDNIGHT WHEN Samuel and Blanche finished making love. He gently kissed her on the forehead. "You've changed my life," he said. "I never thought anything could be this good."

"You're the one who's changed my life, Samuel. But I'm worried about you."

"I'll be all right. I just have to help solve the deaths of all these people."

"I'm not talking about all these crimes," Blanche said softly, caressing his neck. "I'm talking about your losing your job, your psychological well-being."

"It's awful not to have a job," Samuel said, propping himself up on his elbows and looking at her. "But none of this is as bad as my darkest days. I've never told you about them, have I?"

"No, you haven't. Mom told me a little about your parents being murdered, and your having to drop out of college, and I saw how you got ahold of yourself and solved the Chinatown murders."

"There's more to it than that. My parents' murders were bad enough. But what you don't know is what occurred after that. I badly injured a young woman while driving drunk. I could have gone to prison for it, but a young San Francisco lawyer literally saved me from going to the pokey. But I think about that young woman every day, and I have tremendous guilt about her health and her rehabilitation. And, of course, what I did to her was inexcusable."

"That was a long time ago, wasn't it?"

"Yes, it was, but it's still with me."

"Are you in touch with her?"

"Yes, I am."

"How is she doing now?"

"She's still has problems, but she's back to her painting and she and her young son are getting by."

"She's an artist?" asked Blanche.

"Yes, and a very good one from what I understand. She's French."

"Can she physically take care of herself and her child?"

"Oh, yes. He's a lovely boy and the fact that she has him has helped in her rehabilitation."

"Why don't you commit yourself to do something for her, like helping pay to get her established in the art world?"

"That's what I was doing before I got fired."

"Oh, I think I see where the gloom is coming from. What can I do to help you get through this?"

Samuel smiled. "You're doing plenty. I need to get a job and resume taking care of my responsibilities."

"Are you going to take Jim Abernathy up on his offer?"

"Yeah, but not for the reason you think. I'm going to work for him to try and put Conklin in prison for all the harm he's done to so many people."

"So, Samuel the crusader is back!" she laughed. "Now, get some rest." She kissed him and turned out the light.

* * *

The next day, Samuel, Bernardi and Philip Macintosh met

Barney McLeod in his office. Over a cup of coffee, they discussed the Grace Conklin killing.

"Did you find anything at the scene of the crime that will point us in the right direction?" asked Samuel.

"You've been around enough of these to know that we don't know," said Turtle Face. "We pick up everything that looks suspicious and then sift through it all."

"Do you mind if the three of us have a look?" asked Bernardi.

"Not at all. I've spread it out on the conference room table. Come with me." They followed him into another room where several objects were laid out on a white sheet that covered the table.

As Samuel retrieved his notebook, Mac took out his camera and inserted a flash bulb in the socket. "Has everything here been checked for prints?" asked Bernardi.

"Not the way your people would do it. Where the hell were your guys when this was going down?"

"Too many dead people at the same time," said Bernardi. "We just came up short of personnel. I'm sorry about that, but we can't cover them all."

"I understand," said Turtle Face. "I think my investigators did a pretty thorough job. We'll let Mac and Samuel follow through on what else is needed."

"Is this a chunk of blond hair?" asked Samuel, pointing to a few strands lying on an evidence envelope.

"It's synthetic, obviously from a hairpiece," said Turtle Face. "We surmise that it was from a wig or a toupee. But right now we don't know if it's connected to the crime or not."

"Have you figured out if the perpetrator was male or female?" asked Bernardi.

"My guess is that it was a man. A woman wouldn't have the strength to strangle the victim from behind the bench, which is where we think she was sitting. And the ground behind it was trampled by a person weighing more than a hundred and seventy pounds."

"Any footprints?" asked Samuel.

"Unfortunately, none that we can use."

"What's that giant wilted daisy doing there?" asked Samuel.

"Not sure. It was on the ground and seemed out of place, so I had my boys put it in an envelope."

"See how its stem is cut at an angle? If we can find out where it came from, maybe we could work backwards and figure out who bought it."

"Why do you think it's a purchased flower?" asked Mac.

"Because it's too big to be homegrown. It looks like it was juiced with a lot of fertilizer."

"Get a photo of the flower," said Bernardi, "and either you or Samuel, see if you can run down where it came from."

"I'll do it," said Samuel. "I have time on my hands."

"Anything else in that pile that piques your interest?" Bernardi asked the group.

"We picked up several cigarette butts," said Turtle Face.

"How many?" asked Bernardi.

"At least ten, but they're all different brands. One wouldn't think there were that many on the market."

Samuel laughed. "You must not watch much TV or look at the billboards around town. There are so many that it gets confusing, and I don't even smoke anymore."

"Did you find any that were directly under the bench where someone sitting on it would have stamped it out on the ground?" asked Bernardi.

"No such luck. They were all over the place."

"Where did you find this one?" asked Samuel, picking up a Parliament butt with tweezers.

"Hold on," said Turtle Face. "The note says it was found right next to the bench."

"Someone could have flicked it there from the bench," said Samuel.

"No, no," said Turtle Face. "It was stubbed out on the bench. See the photo? It shows where it was put out."

"Any prints on it?"

"They're smeared," said Turtle Face. "If we had some prints to compare them to, maybe. And remember, comparing prints is an arduous process, so even if we could identify a particular pattern, we would be weeks away from a match."

"Maybe the clue is the brand," said Samuel. "I'll start there."

"Why did you pick up the oak leaf?" asked Bernardi.

"We saw it and realized it didn't belong there. So someone must have dropped it. Maybe it fell off the killer's clothes."

As Samuel and Bernardi left the examiner's office, Bernardi noticed that Samuel had a strange look on his face.

"What's bothering you?" he asked.

"It just doesn't add up. I can't put my finger on what's missing right now, but let me give it some thought and we'll talk about it more later."

* * *

That afternoon, Samuel headed to Bernardi's Bryant Street office. As he waited for the detective, he watched the cars zooming by on the adjacent freeway, which led to the Bay Bridge, and considered what they knew so far about the Conklin murder case. When Bernardi arrived, Samuel skipped the small talk and got straight to business.

"I have a plan to canvas the area where Grace Conklin was murdered," said Samuel. "Maybe we can find out what she was doing in that neck of the woods."

"I assumed that you would come up with something and give me some good information, but that's not why I asked you to come by," said Bernardi. "The D.A. is going to trial next week on the bottled water poisonings in Chinatown. I wanted to touch base with you on those cases and hear what you think about the strength of our evidence."

"Twenty-two elderly people dead and proof positive that at least some of them drank arsenic-infected water taken, un-authorized, from the river at the Fort Ross State Park," said Samuel. "It sounds like an open-and-shut case to me."

"The owner of the Flower Blossom Bottling Company, Min Fu-Hok, has hired the same firm that represented Conk-lin in his case," said Bernardi.

"What's his defense?" asked Samuel.

"His attorneys claim that the corporation may be liable, but that he, personally, isn't" said Bernardi.

"Because?"

"They say that whatever he did, he did it within the course and scope of his employment with the company and therefore he can't be personally liable."

"Wasn't he the one who ordered his employees to get the water?" asked Samuel.

"Yeah," said Bernardi, "and according to them, he never ordered any tests on it to see if it was contaminated. The D.A. doesn't think much of the defense or of his lawyers, since the Conklin case is the only other criminal case they've handled in recent years."

"The fireworks start on Monday, huh?"

"That's what the D.A. told me."

"I'll be there," said Samuel.

"Speaking of too many dead people, let's talk a little about the Chad Conklin case," said Samuel. "Anything new on the witness who disappeared?"

"Nah," said Bernardi. "I was hoping that you would pro-vide me with something."

"I have a meeting set up with Jim Abernathy this evening

at Camelot, and he's supposed to give me some information on Conklin that may help us. In addition, a few weeks back he offered me a job. I hope it's still on the table because I'm broke."

"Abernathy just laid his daughter to rest. Do you think he's up for dealing with Conklin so soon after that?"

"He's the one who asked me to meet him," said Samuel. "He must be angry enough to get started."

9

More about Chad Conklin

Samuel and Jim Abernathy met in Melba's office, which was located at the rear of Camelot just behind the hors d'oeuvre table. A polished mahogany door, which creaked under the pressure of the steel spring that secured the latch when it was closed, separated the small room from the rest of the bar. Samuel, who was familiar with the room's layout, made his way in the dark to the desk, which was pushed up against the back wall. He turned on the room's sole source of light, a small desk lamp that that Melba had bought at a secondhand store, its shade adorned with pink ribbon. The soft light illuminated a swiveling secretarial chair in front of the desk and an ordinary kitchen chair set off to one side. The back wall of the office was covered with tarpaper, and various objects hung from the nails on the exposed studs. Samuel indicated to Abernathy that he should sit in the swivel chair and he took the other one.

"Are you sure you're up to this right now?" asked Samuel.

"You bet your sweet ass I am," said Abernathy. "That son of a bitch has been a free man for too long. Let's get him."

"In order to do that I have to find Sambaguita Poliscarpio. And then I have to prove that Conklin was hiding him."

"Hold it, Samuel. Let's start at the beginning. Remember, I promised you a job. Let's say your starting salary is the same as you were getting as a reporter, plus an expense account because you are going to have to do a lot of digging. Does that sound like a fair deal to you?"

"More than fair," said Samuel, smiling. "I accept."

"The next thing I can do is to give you background on this asshole, so you can have a better idea of what makes him tick. I know from reading detective stories that the more you know about a potential criminal, the easier it is to catch him."

"Okay," said Samuel, taking out his notebook and a pen. "Let's start with Conklin's childhood. Where is he from?"

"I learned that he's from Bakersfield. His family came west from Oklahoma during the 1930s Dust Bowl. He was the first person from that clan to even finish high school, let alone graduate from a university. That apparently created a rift with his father, because in Okie hierarchy, he had surpassed the old man."

Abernathy leaned back in his chair, stretching his legs out in front of him. "He was a football star at Berkeley, and was on the 1959 Rose Bowl team that lost to the University of Iowa." A look of sadness crossed his face; the loss of his daughter still showed. "But you probably already know all this, lad."

"Actually, I know next to nothing about him," said Samuel. "Nobody wants to talk about him. It's like he has them all scared."

"Yeah, that's him. But I hired a private detective. That's how I know so much."

Samuel took a deep breath and stretched. "Would you like a drink?"

"Sure, I'll have a Guinness."

Samuel exited into the bar, returning a few minutes later with a Guinness for Abernathy and a Scotch over the rocks for himself. The two clinked glasses.

"Do you have any dirt on him that the cops could use to put pressure on him?" asked Samuel.

"Here's what I've been told. He runs that chemical factory and ships a lot of poison, stuff like DDT and something new called Agent Orange, to the Far East. Because he mixes the chemicals on his property, he has a big problem getting rid of the toxic leftovers."

"You mean like the sludge that the men were working in when the man was killed?"

"Yeah, that stuff shows up every day, from what I'm told."

"What does he do with it?"

"The workers had a toilet out in the yard down by the bay. But they didn't use it to relieve themselves. He made them flush the sludge down the toilet and into the bay. His company was eventually fined for contaminating the bay, so he had the sewer line disconnected and now the sludge just percolates into the ground. The lot is so poisoned that it will probably take a hundred years to clean up, if it's even possible." Abernathy paused, taking another sip of his Guinness.

Samuel had been busily writing in his notebook, but now he stopped and looked up. "That's really important. The health department can shut him down. What he's doing is against the law. He can be prosecuted."

Abernathy smiled cynically. "I would have thought so, but the bastard's still in business, and he seems to have enough friends in high places that he can keep going."

"Does this guy have any redeeming qualities?" asked Samuel.

"One night Grace and I were having cocktails, and I asked her the same question. She was always on guard with me 'cause she knew I didn't like the bastard. But she started crying when she told me that he really loved his mother and that his mother tried to help him when he was fighting to escape the misery of his life in Bakersfield. She would slip him money behind the father's back when he was in college.

"I asked my daughter why she was crying," Abernathy

continued, trying to hold back his own tears. "She told me that she wished he had that kind of affection for her."

Abernathy took out his handkerchief and dabbed at the tears filling his red, swollen eyes. "I'm sorry, it's painful for me to think of my sweet girl being shit on by that asshole."

Samuel nodded. "I understand how you feel. I'm sorry I have to ask you all these questions, but I'm trying to get to the bottom of all that's happened. Do you have any proof that he did her in?"

Even in the dim light of Melba's office, Samuel could see Abernathy's face darken with anger. "If he did it, I still can't figure out his motive. He'd already established himself, with my help, and if he didn't need her anymore as a trophy wife, he could have just walked away. But maybe there was something we don't know, like she had a secret lover and he was jealous. If that was the case, it's another ball game, as you Yanks say. That's what I want you to find out, if this was a jealousy thing. I still don't think he would be so stupid to do it himself. But I have an open mind, and I will spend whatever it takes to find out who killed her."

Samuel flipped through the pages of his notebook until he found what he was looking for. "What about this witness who disappeared, Sambaguita Poliscarpio? Do you know anything about him?"

Abernathy took some papers out of his inside jacket pocket and shuffled through them. "Here's what I found out about him. When Conklin was training as a Navy Seal, Poliscarpio was a steward on the ship that transported the Seals on their training missions. Poliscarpio had been in the Navy for more than twenty years when they met, so he was able to retire and go to work for Conklin. I guess he figured it was time to create a new life for himself, since he had his government pension to fall back on as a cushion if things didn't work out with Conklin."

"Where did Conklin get the money to start his business? From you?"

"I'm embarrassed to say that, in part, he did. But he already had the property where the accident happened."

"How did he get it?"

"He blackmailed a professor at Cal."

"How did he do that?"

"It seems there was a professor who was a kind of mascot to the football team, who used to jack off the football players and get the girls to have sex with them, and Conklin threatened to expose him unless the professor loaned him ten thousand dollars so he could buy the property. He dealt with my daughter the same way. He saw that she came from money, so he went after her. I had a bad feeling about him from the beginning. I tried to stop the relationship, but you know how kids are when they're in love. I'm afraid I only made the situation worse. In fact, my dislike of Conklin is probably the reason they got married."

"The background stuff about his character is good to know," said Samuel, "but if all this information about dumping toxic stuff into the bay turns out to be true, we can get the bastard on that."

"It'll be up to you to prove it," Abernathy said with a smile, getting up and shaking Samuel's hand. "I've set up an office for you at my place in West Oakland. There's a desk and a phone, and you can use my secretarial staff if you need to. Are ye ready to start tomorrow?"

"Yes, sir. I'll be there. What time do you open the doors?"

"The office is available any time after seven," said Abernathy.

* * *

After Conklin's release by the court and pursuant to the

deal he'd made, Samuel settled into a routine at Abernathy's office in West Oakland, going there every day and working diligently at chasing down leads on the disappearance of Conklin's foreman, so that the criminal case against him could go forward. At the same time he kept his sources on alert for any events that could serve his interests as a reporter and earn him a little extra money as a freelancer.

It was Friday morning, November 22, 1963. Samuel was drinking coffee and checking out a rumor he'd heard about the whereabouts of Poliscarpio Sambaguita. He'd just pulled a draft article from his briefcase that was under a deadline when he heard Abernathy's secretary scream. He rushed to the reception desk and saw her holding a piece of the Dow Jones ticker tape in her hand as she sobbed uncontrollably.

"What's wrong, Agnes?" he asked, alarmed.

But all she could do was hand him the piece of tape. It read: President shot in Dallas at approximately 12:30 a.m. local time.

Samuel read and reread it, and then rushed to the machine and saw that it was working overtime. It had stopped giving stock quotes and was in a pile on the floor. He reached down and started reading what was being reported. He noticed he was hyperventilating as he continued to listen to Agnes sob at her desk. He could hardly believe what he was reading.

When Jim Abernathy arrived to find his secretary frozen at her desk in a pool of tears, he asked Samuel what the hell was happening.

"President has just been shot," stammered Samuel.

Abernathy reacted viscerally. "Can't be," he said, shaking his head. "He's the first Irish President. Too much riding on him for that to happen."

Samuel nodded. "I know. But here it is in black and white."

Abernathy rushed to turn on the TV in his office, Samuel

on his heels. On CBS, Walter Cronkite was giving details about what had occurred. Both men stood in front of the set, dumbfounded. At 11:00 a.m., Cronkite confirmed everyone's worst fears. The young President was dead.

Samuel shook his head, and he looked over at Abernathy who had a haunting look of denial in his eyes. "It can't be true," he said.

"I'm not Irish," said Samuel. "But I bet I feel the same way. He was our guy, the first President born in the twentieth century. He represented our hopes and dreams for the future. He was going to finish the job that Roosevelt started, and now I'm afraid it's all over. The crazy ones will say he was too liberal and will squash civil rights, human rights and every other right you can imagine. I think we're in for a terrible time." Abernathy turned the TV off. Both men sat without speaking for several minutes trying to grasp the full magnitude of what had just been reported.

Samuel wiped the tears from his eyes on the sleeve of his khaki sports coat. "I have to get out of here."

"Let's go to Melba's," said Jim. "She'll take care of us."

"Okay," said Samuel.

Abernathy waved to his secretary on the way out. "Come on, Agnes, we need to be among friends," and she followed them out the door.

No one spoke on the drive across the Bay Bridge.

When they arrived at Camelot, there wasn't an inch of space at the horseshoe bar. Melba was behind it, pouring drinks on the house, the make-up on her cheeks smeared with tears. When she saw Samuel and Jim Abernathy she stopped what she was doing and came out to greet them. She hugged Jim and then grabbed Samuel and held onto him, sobbing. In a broken voice she said, "I can't believe this happened."

The crowd was somber and had its collective eye on the television, set above the bar. People looked like zombies watching it as it droned on and on about the tragedy. Some were drinking and others were wiping their tears.

Then Jim Abernathy climbed up on the horseshoe bar and began singing Danny Boy in a beautiful baritone voice and one by one those who knew the words joined in and those who didn't lip-synced it. It turned into a real Irish wake.

10

The People versus Min Fu-Hok

THE DAY OF RECKONING ARRIVED for Min Fu-Hok. The District Attorney's two top trial lawyers answered the presiding judge's call. "The prosecution is ready and estimates the case will take ten trial days."

"The defendant is ready for trial, Your Honor," responded the defendant's lead attorney. "We estimate the defense case will take no more that two days."

"This case is assigned to Judge Hiram Peterson in Department Eight. There will, however, be a slight delay. His department opens at 11 a.m."

Upon the announcement of the judge in the case, a murmur arose among the prosecuting attorney's staff, which was seated in the back of the room. Samuel, who sat with them and was writing an account of the proceedings in his notebook, looked up. "Isn't that the guy who acquitted Chad Conklin?" he asked.

"That's not exactly what happened," said one of the attorneys next to him. "He didn't hold him over for trial in the Superior Court. We all understood we didn't have the evidence. The D.A. and Peterson worked together for years at the U.S. Attorney's Office. The D.A. trusts him to do the right thing. He told us that a challenge wasn't in the cards. It wouldn't look good politically, and if he got mad at us, he could hurt us in other prosecutions. We have a lot of cases on the calendar."

"Why not challenge him every time?" asked Samuel.

"Because there aren't enough judges, and delaying a case causes all kinds of problems with timely trials. If the defense bar knows we are out to get a judge they stop waiving time, hoping they'll get him in case of a delay. And as you know, if the case doesn't go to trial on time, the defendant walks."

* * *

At eleven o'clock the bailiff unlocked Judge Hiram Peterson's courtroom and the defendant, the opposing attorneys and onlookers filled the courtroom. There were more than a hundred people in the room, more than half of them Chinese. This was unusual in the white man's part of town.

Samuel muscled his way in amongst them.

After the crowd quieted down, the clerk entered the courtroom from the rear and placed a file on the dais. Soon after, the bailiff came through the side door and announced the judge. "Hear ye, hear ye, Department Eight of the Superior Court in and for the City and County of San Francisco is now in session, the Honorable Hiram Peterson presiding. Please remain seated."

A tall figure entered the room through the back door, climbed the two steps of the dais and sat down in the brown leather chair. Judge Peterson was as imposing as Samuel remembered, down to his flowing robes, impeccable steel-gray hair and square jaw. The judge picked up a pair of glasses, read from a piece of paper and instructed the clerk to call the case.

The clerk stood up from behind the desk in front of the dais. "The People of the State of California versus Min Fu-Hok," he said, announcing the case number. "Please state your appearances for the record, and give the court a time estimate."

One of the prosecution lawyers rose. "Giuseppe Maximiliano for the People. We estimate ten trial days, Your Honor."

The defense lawyer who had represented Chad Conklin followed. "James Morrison from Pillsbury, Madison and Sutro for the defendant. We estimate two days maximum for the defense—if this case gets even that far." His tone was arrogant and he barely hid a smirk as he sat down.

"Any motions?" asked the court.

"Yes, Your Honor," responded Giuseppe, the lead attorney for the prosecution. "We ask that all potential witnesses be excluded from the courtroom."

"Any objection, Mr. Morrison?"

"None, Your Honor."

"Is that it on the motions?" asked the judge.

After a few moments of silence, the defense attorney stood again. "Your Honor, we have a motion, but we would like it to be heard in chambers."

"Very well," said the judge, "the courtroom will reopen at 2 p.m." He turned to the bailiff. "Call up the jury pool. When we come back this afternoon, the spectators all need to be on the left side of the courtroom. We need the right side for potential jurors." He picked up the file and left the courtroom for his chambers, followed by the two attorneys from the D.A.'s office, the three lawyers representing the defendant and the court reporter.

Later that afternoon Samuel learned from Giuseppe what took place behind closed doors. According to the lawyer, after everyone had crowded into the judge's chambers, the judge addressed the defense attorney. "What can we do for you, Mr. Morrison?"

"The indictment asserts that our client is charged with twenty-two deaths from arsenic poisoning."

"That's what the Grand Jury found," said the judge.

"They can only prove one death, and that's of the elderly lady, Mrs. Chow," said Morrison. "The rest of the indictment is based on circumstantial evidence."

"What is it that you want from the court, Mr. Morrison?"

"We want an order that the prosecution not be permitted to mention the deaths of any other potential poisoning victims unless they have proof to submit to the court, prior to bringing up that particular death, that the person died of arsenic poisoning as a result of drinking Flower Blossom Mineral Water."

"How extensive do you want the order to be?"

"It should provide that they can't bring up the name of a dead person or a particular death while we are picking the jury or during the opening statement. Beyond that, before they attempt to present any evidence of any other death in this case, they have to present evidence to the court outside the presence of the jury that at least shows, prima facie, that that person died as a direct result of drinking the defendant's company's product."

"What's the People's position, Mr. Giuseppe?" asked the judge, taking off his glasses and laying the indictment on his desk.

"That you're on the right track, Judge. The indictment you just put down is the controlling document. It says that Mr. Min is charged with twenty-two homicides as a result of providing arsenic-tainted water to each of the twenty-two victims. That's the law of the case."

The judge raised an eyebrow. "Even without the proof that Mr. Morrison claims is necessary to establish that any of the twenty-two deaths was a result of people being poisoned by the defendant's arsenic-laced mineral water?"

"We already proved to the Grand Jury that they all drank his mineral water, and that they died."

"What about proximate cause?" asked Morrison. "It's still

a legal requirement in this state in order to prove that one action is the cause of another."

"If the people can't prove proximate cause, then the defendant goes free on that particular charge," said Giuseppe.

"Yeah," laughed Morrison cynically. "After they've accused him of killing all the old people of Chinatown."

The judge ran a hand through his hair. "All right, I've heard enough. The matter is submitted. I'll have a ruling before you start picking a jury. You gentlemen grab a bite to eat and we'll see you back here at ten minutes to two this afternoon."

* * *

Giuseppe pushed aside his half-eaten sandwich and the penal code he had been reading and looked over at Samuel and Bernardi. "The son of a bitch may have a point. If we get a conviction on twenty-two counts of manslaughter, Min's lawyers can get the case reversed on appeal because the Grand Jury went ape-shit accusing him of all the deaths when really there wasn't enough evidence. The cremated remains of twenty-one of them didn't have convincing signs of arsenic poisoning."

"Who took it before the Grand Jury?" asked Samuel.

"The D.A. He was pissed that Conklin got off, and let's face it, he knows how to get headlines. Here we have a ruthless Chinese big spender who was fleecing the public, so the D.A. figured he could make him look bad and argue—in the subtext of course—that the white community would have been next if he hadn't been stopped. He was willing to take that chance and make it look as if he were pulling out all the stops when it came to public safety."

"Didn't he think that he would have top legal counsel?" asked Bernardi.

"Sure he did, but you saw the headlines in the papers:

'Chinese Millionaire Accused of Killing 22.' He didn't give a shit because he knew he had public outrage on his side."

"When I read the paper, I thought it was ironic," said Samuel. "You've never heard of anyone getting fired for going after a Chinese businessman with a headline, did you?"

"The publisher would have kicked his lawyers out of his office," said Giuseppe, smiling. "White boys get judged by a different standard. You found that out the hard way."

"It seems that, in the end, Chinese money is as good as any white man's," said Samuel.

"Not so fast. Min Fu-Hok is not out of the woods. In my professional opinion, he's at least facing a conviction for involuntary manslaughter and some jail time, and probably even a fine."

"Any chance of him walking?" asked Bernardi.

"I would say none, but you know the old saying." Giuseppe laughed. "The guy who never lost a case never tried one." He stood up and stretched, picking up the half-eaten sandwich and tossing it in the wastebasket.

* * *

Later, Giuseppe explained to Samuel what happened after the lawyers and the court reporter returned to the judge's chambers just before two that afternoon. Judge Peterson, already in his robe, removed his glasses, setting them atop the casebooks piled on his desk, before addressing the group. Giuseppe noticed an open copy of West's penal code on the judge's side panel.

"Mr. Morrison has a point," said the judge. "We have an indictment here but it is based on pretty flimsy evidence. You won't even get past a non-suit on your opening statement, Mr. Giuseppe. So my ruling is that you can't mention the first twenty-one cases of the cremated decedents when you give your opening statement. And if you are serious about trying to prove that any of them died as a result of drinking Flower Blossom water, then we'll have to have a hearing away from the jury to see if the People can sustain their case, prima facie. Is my ruling clear to both sides?"

"Yes, sir," said Morrison, smiling.

"Yes, sir," Giuseppe answered angrily. "That means we can go forward on only one cause of action."

"Better something than nothing," agreed the judge, smiling.

"Half a loaf, huh?" said Giuseppe, shrugging his shoulders.

"Half a loaf," said the judge. "Let's get to work."

They all stood up and filed out of the judge's chambers and into the courtroom. Giuseppe signaled a thumbs-down to Samuel and Bernardi, who were seated in the first row with the Chang family, on the left side of the courtroom. They grimaced and Samuel leaned over to whisper in Bernardi's ear.

The judge installed himself on the dais and the clerk called the case. The defendant entered the courtroom with an associate of Mr. Morrison. He was a Chinese man of medium height with black hair and a mustache. His well-tailored, dark blue suit and expensive gray silk tie suggested hc was a wealthy man. He sat down at the counsel table next to James Morrison.

"Gentlemen, it is time to start picking a jury. Since I have determined there are two sides, the plaintiff will get thirty preemptory challenges, as will the defendants—that is Mr. Min Fu-Hok and the Flower Blossom Mineral Water Bottling Company."

"Wait a minute, Judge," said a clearly agitated Morrison, standing up, "we have two defendants."

"Your defendants have a unity of interest," the judge said, cutting him short. "The code only provides for what I've given you. Will the clerk call the first twelve jurors?"

"Before we get started, may we approach the bench?" Mr. Morrison asked the judge, still agitated.

"It's not about the same issue, is it?"

"No, sir."

"Very well, approach."

The attorneys gathered at the bench for a heated discussion. "We have a motion that all witnesses be excluded from the court pending their testimony," said Morrison, "yet we see Lieutenant Bernardi and the Chang family in the front row."

"Do you intend to call any of them as witnesses, Mr. Giuseppe?" asked the judge.

"The family for sure, but I don't know about Bernardi. There are other witnesses from the Attorney General's office who gathered the evidence as well."

"If any of them stay in the courtroom, you can't use them," said the judge.

Upon being informed of the judge's order, Bernardi motioned to the Chang family and they left, leaving Samuel behind to brief them on the trial later.

* * *

It took three days to pick a jury of twelve. According to the law, the judge had the right to discharge any juror who he felt could not be fair and impartial. As a result, he excused several people for cause after they admitted they didn't like Chinese people, or even for saying they didn't like Chinese food or culture. This helped the defense since it saved them from using challenges that they otherwise would have had to exercise. The judge also excused potential jurors who said they hated rich people, adding that they would find it impossible to treat them fairly.

Ironically, Giuseppe was forced to challenge several

Italians from North Beach because they admitted to enjoying good working relations with their Chinese business counterparts and to being sympathetic to anyone who had become wealthy as a result of commerce, no matter what his race.

In the end, a jury was empanelled, consisting of eight white men and four white women. Giuseppe indicated to Samuel that he'd gotten as good a cross-section of the white community as there was to get in San Francisco. He'd wanted Chinese Americans on the jury but the defense used all their challenges to keep them off.

Each time the defense peremptorily challenged a potential Chinese juror, Samuel heard grumbling among the many Chinese spectators, although they discussed their displeasure quietly amongst themselves, and the judge never had to pound his gavel. Samuel was equally disapproving, and after court had adjourned, he talked the matter over with Bernardi and Giuseppe.

"It's obvious what those bastards are doing," said Samuel. "The defendant is supposed to have his case heard by a jury of his peers. That's not happening here. Anybody with even a whiff of being anti-business is kicked off either because they admit it or they're asked a trick question that compromises them."

"How does it look to you?" Bernardi asked Giuseppe.

"Not great, but better than a zero," was all he would say. "The jury is not the problem."

* * *

The first day of the trial went as expected. Giuseppe delivered an opening statement promising that the People would prove that the bottled water from the Flower Blossom Mineral Water Bottling Company was tainted with arsenic, that the owner had told his workers where to procure the water and that the owner had never set in place any procedure to check the quality of the water. After bottling, the prosecution said, he sold the tainted water and Mrs. Chow died as a result of drinking it.

The defense argued that Mrs. Chow's death was an unfortunate accident that, at most, was due to simple negligence rather than reckless criminal conduct and that the defendant Min Fu-Hok himself was innocent of wrongdoing.

The prosecution then proceeded to present the evidence promised in its opening statement. Jack Bruschet of the California Attorney General's office described the scene when he arrived at the Flower Blossom Mineral Water Bottling Company with a cease and desist order, and provided the names of the employees found hiding behind the water tanks, thanks to Melody Song, who had acted as interpreter.

Phillip Macintosh gave an analysis of the high concentration of arsenic found in the water stored in the company's bottles and the three tanks. He also testified that the water matched samples taken from Fort Ross State Park.

The medical examiner confirmed that Mrs. Chow's death resulted from consuming the arsenic-tainted water found in the Flower Blossom bottles discovered in the Changs' apartment.

Later, several Flower Blossom employees testified that they had procured the water used by the company from Fort Ross State Park, pursuant to instructions given to them by the owner, Min Fu-Hok. All testified that the owner had told them that if they were caught, they were to explain that the water was being taken for irrigation purposes.

Next up was Huang Wang, the Flower Blossom foreman, who appeared under California Evidence Code 776 as a hostile witness. He was short and slightly overweight, with black bushy hair and a pockmarked face. After the witness, who only spoke Chinese, was sworn in through a Chinese interpreter, Giuseppe began to question him. However, after giving his name and place of birth and naming his citizenship, the witness invoked his rights under the Fifth Amendment to the United States Constitution, and refused to answer any more questions.

Giuseppe was thrilled with the witness's performance because it suggested that the defendants had something to hide.

The last witnesses called by the prosecution were Mr. and Mrs. Chang. They told the jury of the circumstance of Mrs. Chow's death, and Mrs. Chang explained how she had happily taken care of her elderly mother and what a wonderful contribution she had been to the Chang family. During her testimony, several of the jurors wiped their eyes, using tissues provided by the bailiff.

When Mrs. Chang finished her testimony, the prosecution rested.

The defense's approach was a surprise. The first witness was the water company's lawyer. He confirmed that he had filed the papers forming the corporation some five years before. The filings and the by-laws showed there were three corporate directors. According to his testimony, the same people named in the original filings were still on the board and running the company. Later, they took the witness stand and confirmed those facts.

The defense authenticated several sets of corporate minutes from various company meetings that showed that the board of directors, which consisted of three prominent businessmen from Chinatown, met every three months, from the date of incorporation to the present. Included in the minutes was a provision that any and all of President Min Fu-Hok's actions carried out in the ordinary course and scope of his employment—which included procuring water from whatever source was available—were automatically ratified by the board of directors.

As promised by Min's lawyers, the defense only took two days. Min himself did not take the stand, as was his right. He could and did remain silent, although his minions painted a picture of an executive who was far removed from the company's core business. With that testimony the defense rested.

"Since both sides have rested," the judge told the jury, "I am going to excuse the members of the jury until tomorrow morning. At that time, both sides will give closing arguments and we hope to have this case to you by tomorrow afternoon."

The judge then reminded the jury of the rules. "Remember, you are not to talk to anyone about this case until you are sequestered in the jury room," he said. "That will be after I give you instructions on the law of this case."

The jury filed out and the judge addressed counsel. "I will see you in chambers after lunch, when we'll go over instructions."

Over lunch in Bernardi's office, Samuel queried Giuseppe about the defense's tactics. "What do you think Morrison is up to?"

"It's pretty obvious. He's going to argue that the corporation is responsible but that the man isn't. That's why he introduced all those minutes."

"Do you think the jury will buy that crap?" asked Bernardi.

"Some of it depends on what instructions he convinces the judge his client is entitled to."

"How has the judge conducted himself?" asked Bernardi

"From a layman's point of view," said Samuel, "I'd say he acts like a real judge."

Giuseppe laughed. "I agree. So far he's been right on with all his rulings. Let's see what he does with the instructions."

* * *

Samuel and Giuseppe met again at the end of the day, when Giuseppe gave Samuel the court reporter's transcript of what went on when the lawyers gathered in the judge's chambers that afternoon. He explained that there was sharp disagreement between the lawyers about what instructions should be given.

Samuel read the transcript, curious to see what had happened, and Giuseppe filled in details as needed. The first thing Samuel read was an account of the judge stepping in to take charge of the squabbling lawyers:

"You're all acting like school boys. Let's go about this in an orderly fashion. The first question we need to answer is if there should be an instruction on Murder 1 or Murder 2. I'm sure neither of you think those are appropriate, so I will give neither. That brings us to voluntary and involuntary manslaughter. Mr. Morrison, what do you have to say about those two instructions?"

"I think that both of those instructions are fine against the Flower Blossom Mineral Water Bottling Company, but neither should be given against our individual client, Mr. Min Fu-Hok."

"That's a crock, Judge!" Giuseppe interjected. "There's no way to insulate Mr. Min from this crime. He and his company should hang together, as the old saying goes."

"Let's hear Mr. Morrison out," the judge responded. "Finish your thought, Mr. Morrison."

"It's simple, Your Honor. Mr. Min was only the agent of the corporation. All his actions were done on behalf of the company and the board of directors ratified those actions. He shouldn't be found guilty of anything. Those minutes make that abundantly clear."

"What about that argument, Mr. Maximiliano?" asked the judge.

"It doesn't hold water, Judge, if you'll pardon the pun. Min sent his employees up to Fort Ross so he wouldn't have to pay for purified water, and he never bothered to have the Fort Ross water analyzed to find out if it was safe. That was reckless conduct, and the jury should be allowed to evaluate it. Mr. Morrison's argument applies to the company's wage earners, who were just following Min's instructions. It doesn't make any sense to say that Min can't be charged because the corporation agreed that he was its agent and ratified his conduct. That only means that the corporation is guilty, too."

"What's the purpose of forming a corporation?" Morrison asked rhetorically. "It's to limit liability. That's what happened here. Mr. Min should be protected because he was acting within the course and scope of his employment with the company. He shouldn't be punished for it—that's not what the law intended."

"I repeat, Judge, the employees should be protected, but not him," responded Giuseppe. "The idea of the limitation of liability for a corporation is a civil concept. It wasn't intended to apply in a criminal case. If it were, there would be a myriad of potential felons running around massacring the public with more impunity than they already have. Min's the one who thought up the scheme. If one of his employees died because he drank some of the poisoned water, Min would be liable for civil damages even though workers' compensation should, in theory, be the employee's only remedy."

Morrison answered that even if Min were guilty of gross negligence, that wouldn't be enough to convict him of manslaughter. He said although that would mean Min could be sued in civil court, this particular case was in the criminal system.

"Let the jury decide his fate," said Giuseppe.

As Samuel skimmed the transcript, Giuseppe explained that the judge told the lawyers to continue with the remaining instructions, and that he'd make up his mind on the issue later.

According to the transcript, the group returned to the pivotal question of agency after a short break. "I think Mr. Maximiliano is correct," said the judge. "The idea of a corporation's officer being immune from liability is a civil concept. It doesn't or shouldn't apply to a criminal proceeding. If I'm wrong, and he's convicted, the appellate court will set us straight. So I'm not giving your instruction, Mr. Morrison. Does that take care of everything?"

While Giuseppe answered in the affirmative, the defense attorney responded that he would need to review his client's options. According to Giuseppe, he then stormed out of the room, followed by his two associates.

"Final arguments begin at ten," the judge called after them, just before the door slammed shut. "Each side will get two hours."

* * *

At ten the next morning, the court was called to order. The courtroom was packed, not just the Chang family but also with the families of the other victims who had died after drinking what was widely believed to be arsenic-tainted water. Samuel and Buck Teeth sat in the front row.

Morrison stood up. "Your Honor, the defense has a motion. Can we be heard outside the presence of the jury?"

"Certainly," the judge responded. "Ladies and gentlemen of the jury, we need to have a consultation with the attorneys. It will only take a few moments. The bailiff will escort you to the jury room."

Once they were gone, the judge addressed counsel. "You may proceed, Mr. Morrison."

"In light of your ruling, denying our requested instruction on agency, we move to reopen the defense case and put on the evidence."

Giuseppe was on his feet. "We object, Your Honor. The defense rested its case and is not even claiming it has newly discovered evidence. It just gambled and lost."

"What say you to that, Mr. Morrison?"

"We frankly didn't expect your ruling, and if we had, we would have put on additional evidence."

"But to Mr. Maximiliano's point. You've discovered nothing new in the last twelve hours, correct?"

"That's true, Your Honor. We are not claiming that."

"Then your motion is denied. Bailiff, bring in the jury. Gentlemen, it's time for argument. As I stated yesterday afternoon, each side has two hours. The prosecution goes first, then the defense. And, of course, the prosecution gets the last word. After you are both finished, I will give the legal instructions to the jury so they can begin their deliberations."

The jury filed in and took their seats on one side of the courtroom. Giuseppe went to the podium and once again laid out the evidence, reminding them that he had proved everything he promised in his opening statement.

The defense claimed that while the company certainly bore some blame, Min Fu-Hok did not. It repeated the same argument that had been made to the judge the afternoon before, reiterating that Min was simply an agent of the company. The corporation, rather than its owner, he said, should be found guilty of involuntary manslaughter because its employees had used arsenic-tainted water for its mineral water, which he agreed had caused Mrs. Chow's death.

When Giuseppe retook the podium, he ridiculed Morrison's position, arguing that both the corporation and the owner, Min Fu-Hok, were liable for voluntary manslaughter. He said that Min, only interested in making a profit, had ignored the common-sense safety rules of water purification. Both Min and the company should be convicted of the more serious crime, Giuseppe said, adding that a reckless disregard for public safety was the real cause of Mrs. Chow's death.

When the attorneys finished their arguments, the judge instructed the jury on the law, and the group retired to the jury room to deliberate.

The jury was out only two hours, a fact that filled the courtroom with the buzz of excited speculation as the spectators took their seats. When the jury filed in and sat down, seasoned court observers noted a middle-aged man holding a piece of paper in his hand—an indication that he was the foreman.

When the jury was in place, the judge, seated on the dais, cleared his throat. "Has the jury reached a verdict?" he asked.

The foreman said it had. The clerk walked to the edge of the jury box and the foreman handed him the white sheet of paper, which the clerk then handed to the judge. After the judge read it, he passed it back to the clerk, who announced the verdict.

"We the jury in the above-entitled case find the defendant Min Fu-Hok guilty of voluntary manslaughter."

The crowd broke into excited discussion, clearly supportive of the verdict, and the judge pounded his gavel. "Order in the court! We're in the middle of judicial proceedings." The defendant stared ahead, stone-faced. His attorney bowed his head.

The clerk continued reading. "We the jury in the above-entitled case find the defendant the Flower Blossom Mineral Water Bottling Company, a corporation, guilty of voluntary manslaughter."

There was more noise from the crowd but not enough this time to provoke the judge to call for order.

"Are these your verdicts?" he asked the jury.

"Yes, Your Honor," responded the foreman.

"We would like the jury polled, Your Honor," said Morrison. Criminal case verdicts needed to be unanimous, and were one juror to state that he or she disagreed with the outcome, the defense would have grounds to call for a mistrial.

"Very well," said the judge. "Will the clerk please poll the jury."

Armed with a pen and yellow legal pad, the clerk asked the jurors one by one if each agreed with the verdicts. They all answered in the affirmative.

The judge removed his glasses and turned to address the jury. "Ladies and gentlemen of the jury, you are now excused. The oath of silence that bound you during the trial is over, and you may now speak to anyone you choose about the case. The City and County of San Francisco thanks you for your service."

Samuel and Buck Teeth rushed over to Giuseppe and Samuel shook his hand. "Masterful job. Min and his company got exactly what they deserved. Bernardi will be happy to hear about this. One more bad guy put away. I wish I had a byline so I could inform the public."

"That will happen very soon for you, Mr. Hamilton," said Buck Teeth. "Maybe when word gets out about this case."

Samuel shook his head sadly. "Yeah, sure."

The judge pounded his gavel. "Let's have some order, please! Will the defendant rise? Mr. Min Fu-Hok, you've been convicted of a felony. The bailiff will now take you into custody and hold you there until the date set for sentencing. Will the clerk please tell us when that will be?"

"Your Honor, may I be heard?" said Morrison. "The defendant has no prior criminal record. We request that he be allowed free on the present bail, until sentencing."

"How much is the present bail?" asked the judge.

"Ten thousand dollars."

"The prosecution objects, Your Honor. Mr. Min has been found guilty of a felony. Besides, he's a Chinese national and thus a flight risk. He should be held without bail."

"Gimme a break," said Morrison. "Where can he run to, Communist China? I doubt that."

"Anything else to say on the subject, Mr. Maximiliano?"

"No, Your Honor."

"Bail will be increased to one hundred thousand dollars."

"Thank you, Your Honor," said Morrison with an arrogant smile. "We'll post it right now."

11

The Bloodhound in Him

SAMUEL SAT ACROSS FROM Jim Abernathy in the latter's spacious office. "Have you had any luck finding this Poliscarpio character?" Abernathy asked.

"Not yet, but I have a lead. It's a connection to the workers' compensation insurance carrier," said Samuel. "The woman I spoke to told me she would have something for me by Monday. Unfortunately, Conklin's bookkeeper disappeared with the company records, which makes finding company documents difficult."

"I thought I was the one that was supposed to give you the connections. How did you find this person?"

Samuel laughed. "Being a reporter does give me advantages. And I use as many as I can to get information."

Abernathy laughed and took a sip of his coffee. "My hat's off to ya, Samuel. Anything else of interest in our case?"

"I found two Conklin Chemical workers who are sterile," said Samuel. "Medical testing proved it. I gave their names to Bernardi, and I have a friend who can help them. He's the lawyer that Bernardi's girlfriend, Marisol, works for. The workers can also provide evidence that Poliscarpio ordered them to work without protective gear. Unfortunately, they're no help with Conklin, since they never saw him."

The Halls of Power

On Monday morning, Samuel started his search as soon as he could get someone to answer the phone at the workers' compensation carrier's San Francisco headquarters.

"Hello, Carol," he said, once he'd been put through. "This is your old pal, Samuel. Remember, I'm the guy with cursed spite, and I have to set it right. Do you have anything for me?"

"Oh, yes, the poet and famous reporter. I've been working overtime for you. If anything comes of this, you are going to owe me big time."

"I always pay my debts." Samuel laughed.

"I'm sorry to tell you, but your friend Sambaguita Poliscarpio, if that's the way you pronounce his name, doesn't show up anywhere. I've checked all the patient accounts and all hospital admissions for Conklin Chemical, and no dice. Other than his ambulance ride to San Francisco General Hospital that you already know about, there's no record of him in our files."

"Shit! This doesn't sound promising."

"I did find something suspicious, though," Carol said, cracking her gum.

"What is it?"

"There's a payment made every month to a rest home under the Conklin Chemical Company account, but it is not for Sambaguita Poliscarpio. It's for a Pedro Rivas. Does that help you?"

"Hold on," said Samuel. He pulled a list of Conklin employee names from his pocket. There was no Pedro Rivas listed. "Where does the payment go?"

She gave him the street address of the Morning Sky Rest Home in Stockton, California. After assuring her he would be back in touch, Samuel thanked her and hung up.

He headed straight to Bernardi's office. The aluminum windows were open, and the sound of rushing traffic from the nearby freeway filled the room. Samuel laid his notebook down and pointed to the open page. "I was just given an address where Conklin Chemical's workers' compensation insurance company sends a check for the care of an employee who doesn't exist. But in order to find out if it's Poliscarpio, we have to go to Stockton."

"This is something we should attend to right away," said Bernardi. "What's your schedule look like for the rest of the day?"

"Me? You've got to be kidding. Let's get moving. It takes about two and a half hours. If we're lucky, we can get a statement from him, or you can arrest him."

"I can't arrest him because he hasn't been charged with anything, but I may be able to take him into custody as a material witness. Let me check with the district attorney's office. In that case, we'll have to make arrangements to have a warrant issued by Stanislaus County, and we'll need one of their sheriffs to accompany us to serve it. So we won't be able to leave until tomorrow at the earliest."

* * *

The Morning Sky Rest Home was housed in a large, pumpkin-colored stucco building with a clay-tiled roof. Its asphalt parking lot was big enough for fifty cars. Bernardi, Samuel and a sheriff's deputy showed up with a warrant for the arrest of Sambaguita Poliscarpio as a material witness.

The rest home had no record of Sambaguita Poliscarpio ever having been there, and the manager asked them to leave. With that, the deputy demanded to search the premises, showing the manager the warrant and his badge.

After figuring out what was in store for him if he

continued to stonewall, the manager took only a few seconds before agreeing to cooperate.

"We need you to lead us to the room of an injured Filipino man with a mustache who is in pretty bad shape," said the deputy. "Even though you insist he is not here and never has been."

"We have information he was parked here under the name of Pedro Rivas," added Bernardi.

The manager looked around furtively and lowered his voice. "Is this confidential?"

"Of course," Bernardi lied.

"This man called Pedro Rivas is no longer here. But I may be able to help you." He picked up his phone and dialed a number. "Have Angelina come to the office," he barked.

After a couple of minutes, a small, attractive Mexican woman wearing a white nurse's uniform came into the office. "This is Angelina," the manager said. "She may have information for you."

"You need to talk to these people," he told her in Spanish. "They are the law."

The woman looked frightened.

"We're not going to hurt you or arrest you," Bernardi assured her, "but we need information concerning the whereabouts of Sambaguita Poliscarpio. Do you know where he is?"

Angelina stared at her boss in confusion.

"You have to tell them if you know something," he told her.

"But I promised I would say nothing," she protested in broken English.

"We are from the San Francisco Police Department," Bernardi said. "It is very important that we find this man and speak with him. He is a witness to a crime."

The manager spoke to her again in Spanish, and her

expression changed to fear.

"What did you just say to her?" asked Samuel.

"I told her that if she didn't talk, the police would take her away and jail her until she did."

"That's not exactly true," said Bernardi, "but it's true enough that I won't object. Tell her to start talking."

The manager addressed her again in Spanish.

"What did you say this time?"

"I told her you mean business and she would have to tell you what she knew."

Angelina replied in rapid Spanish. "There was such a man here until two weeks ago," the manager translated. "He is very ill. He has great difficulty breathing. He needs oxygen to stay alive."

"What happened to him?" Samuel asked.

"Two men came one night during her shift and moved him. They didn't say where they were taking him. She was very close to the man, having been with him at night when he needed the most care. He sent her a note with his new address and asked her to forward any mail that came to him in the name of Pedro Rivas or...I can't pronounce the other name."

Angelina showed them a piece of paper with the name SAMBAGUITA POLISCARPIO printed on it, along with the name and address of a rest home called Mountain Crest, which was located on the other side of Stockton.

* * *

Mountain Crest consisted of a group of mobile homes in the middle of nowhere, painted in pastel colors to blend in with the artichoke fields. Samuel, Bernardi and the sheriff's deputy found a man matching Sambaguita Poliscarpio's description on the porch of the rest home, an oxygen tank strapped to his wheelchair. His black hair and mustache were streaked with gray, and he was pale and gaunt. The deputy pushed aside the nurse attending to him. "We're here to serve this warrant on you, Mr. Poliscarpio," said the deputy,

"Leave me alone!" Poliscarpio wheezed, laboring to breathe.

"You have too much information, sir," said Bernardi. "You can make it easy and talk to us as representatives of the law. You can help us out. In any event, though, you are going to have to talk to the Grand Jury about what you know."

"Why should I help you?" Policarpio asked in a raspy, almost inaudible voice.

Samuel told him what they had learned in the investigation, including that Conklin knew the masks were defective. "But he's blaming you," Samuel lied, "saying you gave Carlos and Roberto the masks."

Poliscarpio's pallid face flushed red with anger.

"Roberto told us everything except how you got so fucked up," continued Samuel. "I bet you didn't do this to yourself."

Poliscarpio struggled to breathe as he spoke. "I was warned you were looking for me. That is why I was moved."

"Does your boss know you are here?" Samuel asked.

"Sure," he wheezed. "He and Mr. Spekenworth put me here so you couldn't find me."

"Who is Spekenworth?" asked Samuel.

"He is Mr. Conklin's investigator from back East. He is the one who keeps moving me around. He also told me to keep my mouth shut. But I just want to get this over with. I'm a sick man."

Bernardi explained that Poliscarpio, as a material witness to a homicide, needed to return with them to San Francisco, and that from that moment on, he would be in the protective custody of the San Francisco Police Department. He would be taken to San Francisco General Hospital, where he would be attended to until he was able to testify before the Grand Jury.

After receiving permission from Poliscarpio, Bernardi taped his statement, which took more than two hours. Poliscarpio had to stop and rest several times, and even then, his labored breathing could be heard on the tape.

"You look worn out," said Bernardi, turning off the tape recorder. "It's time for us to get moving. We can't get your wheelchair in my car, but your oxygen tank will fit, and I promise they'll take good care of you at the hospital."

"This will be a relief," Poliscarpio whispered, wiping a tear from his hollowed-out cheek. "I am fed up with hiding."

On the way back to San Francisco, Samuel peppered him with additional questions, his tape recorder running. The witness answered to the extent his health permitted, and by the time they reached the hospital, Samuel and Bernardi had a pretty full picture of what had happened that fateful day at Conklin Chemical.

"Looks like you'll get your job back pretty quick now," Bernardi told Samuel once Poliscarpio was safely in custody in the hospital police ward.

"Do you think I'd ever go back to work for those assholes?" Samuel responded. "As soon as you go to the Grand Jury and give me the all-clear, I'm going to sell this story to the afternoon paper and see if they'll hire me full time."

* * *

Samuel, Abernathy and Melba were seated at the Round Table. Melba and Abernathy were sharing a Lucky Strike, and after passing the cigarette back to her, Abernathy raised his glass to Samuel. "You got that bastard, Samuel," he said, taking a swig. "Here's to ya."

"I'm sorry that's all I got," said Samuel. "Nothing so far proves that Conklin killed your daughter."

"If he's the one who did it, something will come up. I have

enough Fey for that."

Melba laughed. "That Fey thing, it's Irish. Don't hold your breath."

"You can call it whatever you want," said Abernathy, "but you work the same way, baby."

Ignoring him, Melba took a pull on her beer and lit another cigarette.

"When do you start your new job?" she asked Samuel.

"The witness has given his testimony to the Grand Jury and I have a copy of his recorded statement, so I'm not restrained by any confidentiality rules," said Samuel. "Here's a copy of my article." He unfolded a draft of the story. "This is the headline I've crafted, but you know the copy room, the editor may make it more graphic." Melba and Abernathy craned their necks to read the bold type:

Millionaire Caught Redhanded
Hiding Witness to a Crime

Underneath the headline was the story of Conklin's illegal sequestration of Sambaguita Poliscarpio. The article covered three columns of the front page of the afternoon newspaper, Samuel's new employer. Abernathy beamed as Samuel read the details of the article out loud to his small audience.

Part 2

12

Mr. Song's Dream

AT HALF PAST TEN, WHEN the hearing was set to begin, the judge had yet to take the bench. The courtroom was packed, and not just with the usual gang of legal drama watchers who hung around the criminal courts. On this day, it seemed as though half the population of Chinatown had crowded into the room, all waiting to hear what sentence Judge Peterson would hand down to Min Fu-Hok. Many of the spectators were dressed in a myriad of styles reflecting their places of origin throughout southern China; others wore Western garb. The room hummed with the rising and falling tones of the Cantonese dialect.

The defendant sat with his attorney, Morrison, while Giuseppe, the prosecutor, sat alone at his table near the jury box. As the clerk fiddled with paperwork, the bailiff, seated next to the door to the cell where prisoners were held, read the morning paper.

Samuel and Buck Teeth had claimed seats in the front row behind the barrier. They were chatting about the case when the bailiff, setting aside his newspaper and standing up, called the court to order and announced the judge.

Judge Peterson, carrying a large file and two legal casebooks, entered through the back door. He climbed the stairs to the dais, adjusted his robe and sat down. "Call the case," he told the clerk.

"People of the State of California versus Min Fu-Hok."

The prosecuting attorney stood up. "Giuseppe Maximiliano for the People."

"James Morrison for the defendant."

"I see your client is present," said the judge. "Is there any reason why sentence should not be carried out?"

Min Fu-Hok, wearing a neatly pressed gray sharkskin suit and an understated blue tie, rose to address the judge. "No, Your Honor," he said in accented English.

"What is it that the People recommend?" asked the judge.

"We feel that the maximum sentence is appropriate in this case," said Giuseppe. "That is also what the probation report recommends."

"Do the People feel there are any mitigating circumstances that would justify a lighter sentence?" asked the judge.

"Absolutely none," answered Giuseppe, twisting a piece of loose paper from the yellow legal block in front of him. "Mr. Min has shown a callous disregard for our citizens' health and safety. His only interest was hoodwinking the public so he could make money. He has shown absolutely no contrition for the harm he caused."

The judge nodded. "Mr. Morrison, what do you have to say on behalf of your client?"

The defense attorney stood slowly, taking time to adjust his tie. Pushing aside his notes, he looked squarely at the judge. "The maximum sentence in this case would be a travesty of justice, Your Honor. To lock this man up would make no sense. Contrary to the probation report, he has indeed shown contrition, as well as having made a large contribution to the Chinatown YMCA so that it can expand its building site. Aside from this unfortunate accident, Mr. Min has a stellar reputation in the community, as witnessed by the number of character letters recited in the report. We ask that you grant him probation so he can continue his business, which provides jobs for his people and taxes for the City and County of San Francisco and the State of California."

"Mr. Maximiliano?" asked the judge.

"A remarkable request, Judge. It would be unheard of to grant this man probation in light of the evidence. All that was involved here was greed, pure and simple. He even tried to pass the crime off on his corporation, taking no personal responsibility for what he did."

"What about the fine? How much should it be?"

"The People say that it should be at least the amount of his bail—a hundred thousand dollars."

"What say you to all this, Mr. Morrison?"

"My client thinks a hundred thousand is fair if he's grant-ed probation."

"All right, gentlemen, I'm going to take a ten minute recess."

Samuel glanced at his watch, which read eleven o'clock. The judge gathered the file and his law books and exited the courtroom through the same door he had entered.

"What do you think?" asked Samuel.

"This rat should go to jail," said Buck Teeth. "Just look around the courtroom. Too many of these people have been devastated by what this monster did. Plus, the jury found him guilty."

"I agree," said Samuel. "Now let's see what the judge will do with this."

After ten minutes the back door opened and the judge reemerged, the file in one hand and his glasses in the other. He bounded up the steps to the dais as the bailiff called the court to order.

Sitting down, the judge placed his glasses on the blotter in front of him. "Is the defendant ready?"

"Yes, Your Honor," answered Morrison.

"Are the People ready?"

"Yes, Your Honor," answered Giuseppe.

"I have heard this case and I have read the probation report. I have listened to the arguments of counsel and I have given this case many hours of thought. It is the considered opinion of the court that the defendant Min Hok-Fu be granted probation for a period of five years. He is to immediately report to the probation officer in charge of his case and give the department any and all information requested of him. The department will continue to hold his passport during the course of his probation, so he cannot leave the country. If, during its course, he plans to participate in any business having to do with disseminating food or drink to the public, he must request and be granted clearances from the City and County of San Francisco Department of Health. In addition, he is to immediately pay the court a fine in the amount of one hundred thousand dollars."

There was stunned silence as the judge slammed his gavel and left the courtroom. Min Fu-Hok would walk out the courtroom a free man. Giuseppe turned and looked at Samuel in astonishment. Buck Teeth began to cry. Samuel tried to comfort her but it was no use. It was as if a heavy darkness engulfed the room. Then, as the initial shock of the sentence wore off, the crowd began to stir, murmuring its disapproval. Within minutes, disbelief had been transformed into indignation, and then into fury.

Samuel pulled Buck Teeth towards him. "What are they saying?"

"They can't believe this has happened in the United States of America," she said. "They say they came to this country to find justice and look what has happened. The villain has gone free. They don't feel safe."

Within minutes the weeping and shouting grew so loud that deputy sheriffs were called to the courtroom. Prominent citizens of Chinatown pushed their way in and urged the crowd to quiet down, warning that they would be removed otherwise. With that, the crowd began to file out into the hallway, but they didn't quiet down.

"I've never seen so many angry Chinese people," Samuel said.

Buck Teeth nodded. "I know. I'm going to take a cab and let Mr. Song know what's happened here today. He will not be happy."

"I'd like to go with you," said Samuel. "I'll include his comments in my story for this afternoon's paper."

"My hunch is he won't have anything to say today, but give him some time. I doubt if he'll just keep quiet and do nothing."

"So, I should just leave him alone for now?"

"Yes," she answered. "If he says anything, I will call you. In the meantime, work on your story. I think I can promise you he won't take this lying down."

* * *

The phone rang continuously at the offices of the afternoon paper, Samuel's new place of employment. When Melody called—Samuel was surprised to find he was starting to think of her by her given name rather than Buck Teeth—he was down the hall getting a drink of water, and he rushed back to his office to answer the phone. She insisted that she needed to see him in person, so they agreed to rendezvous at Chop Suey Louie's.

Samuel grabbed a notebook and put it in his jacket pocket, checked to make sure he had a ballpoint pen and rushed out to Market Street, where he hailed a cab.

When he arrived at Louie's, Melody was waiting for him on the sidewalk. Instead of her school uniform, she wore a skirt and silk blouse. Samuel smiled at her and they entered the restaurant. Louie's widow was behind the cash register, beside which stood the new aquarium that had been installed after Louie's death. Samuel pointed to one of the tables near the window and put up two fingers. After they were seated, Louie's wife brought a pot of tea, two cups and a menu.

"You must have something really important to tell me," Samuel said.

"I do," she answered. "Yesterday, after court, I went to my uncle's shop and told him what happened. He didn't say a word; he just listened. This morning he called me at home and asked me to come to his shop right away. When I arrived, he was not his usual calm self. He was really agitated. He sat me down in his back room, the one where you were hypnotized for your smoking addiction, and he told me that he'd had a very disturbing dream the night before and wanted to consult me on its significance."

"What was the dream?"

"He told me he was so disturbed by the news I gave him that he had to take a combination of herbs to fall asleep. About four in the morning he awoke to find his bedchamber full of smoke or white vapor. He said there was a lot of noise and an intense white light that lasted almost an hour. But just as rapidly as the cloud appeared, it disappeared, as if sucked out by a vacuum. And the room was completely silent. It was then that he opened his eyes or woke up, he's not sure which."

"What do you think it was?" asked Samuel.

"He told me it was the spirits of the dead people who were poisoned by Min Hok-Fu. He said they came to him as a mass of wailing and murmuring spirits, all trying to express themselves in poignant, anguished whispers. They were asking for justice—the justice that had been denied them by the court."

"That was a powerful dream," said Samuel. "And a pretty tall order. What does he think he can do?"

"Have you forgotten Judge Dee? He can set up a tribunal and try Min Hok-Fu. It's a traditional form of Chinese justice for the victims."

Samuel raised an eyebrow. "I see. Obviously no double jeopardy, but isn't having that kind of a trial a form of vigilantism?"

"Depends on one's point of view, I suppose. The concept dates back to the sixth century. People count on the official system to protect them, but when it doesn't, they feel it's important to take matters into their own hands. My uncle feels that the dream represented the victims' spirits demanding the justice the American system denied them."

"Do you want me to write about this in the paper?"

"Of course not. But Mr. Song and I both want you to know that he will conduct a proceeding to allow the victims' families to air their grievances against Mr. Min Hok-Fu. If the Chinese community finds him guilty, this will show him that he can't get away with what he has done."

"Will Min Hok-Fu be represented by a lawyer?"

"It will have to be a Chinese person who is familiar with how Mr. Song's system works, though not necessarily a lawyer."

"Is there such a person in Chinatown?" asked Samuel.

"Oh, yes. The custom is quite old and there are many wise men in the community who can act as his counsel, if they chose to do so."

"What would stop them?"

"The gravity of his crimes."

"What am I supposed to do with this information if I can't publish it? Can I share it with Bernardi?"

She grimaced. "No. Not yet. Right now this is just between you, me and Mr. Song. He wants you to be an outside witness."

"What happens if the community finds Min guilty? Would they condemn him to death and then kill him? That would be a vigilante killing and a crime under our justice system. Have you thought about that?"

"It's out of my hands, Samuel. You need to ask Mr. Song all these questions."

"Why me?"

She smiled, her braces sparkling as the light hit them. "Because my uncle trusts you. And in exchange, he will help you solve the white man's mystery."

"What does that mean?"

"He will soon have a meeting with you and will explain himself. Right now, you are sworn to secrecy."

"For how long?"

"Until Chinese justice is served."

"I can't make this deal with you," Samuel protested. "I have to talk to Mr. Song directly."

"He will explain everything to you soon," said Melody. "Until then, mum's the word."

"Of course," said Samuel. "Should I come to the shop?"

"Yes. When he is ready, that's where he will meet you, and you will be surprised what he can offer you in return for being a witness to these proceedings. No white man has ever been in the inner circle before, you know."

Samuel nodded, thinking that Melody had grown up so much recently. She looked and acted more like a young lady than a precocious schoolgirl.

13

What's the Daisy Got to Do with It?

SAMUEL SAT ACROSS THE TABLE from Bernardi at the medical examiner's office, the evidence from Grace Conklin's murder scene spread on the white cloth. Bernardi held the photo of the wilting daisy and compared it the now-shriveled flower on the table.

"What the hell does this giant flower have to do with the girl's death?" he asked.

"I have a hunch about that flower," said Samuel. "I'm going to snoop around and see if I can find out who sells giant daisies in the area, and if anyone remembers a blond man purchasing one or a bunch on the day she was killed."

"That's a long shot," said Bernardi.

"What? That it's connected to the killer?"

"No. Not that. That somebody could possibly remember the person who bought a bunch of daisies that day. And even if you hit the jackpot, so what? How are we going to find that person?"

"You've taught me never to jump a step. Let's see if my hunch pays off and someone does remember selling a bunch to a man with blond hair on that day."

"I wouldn't be that specific," said Bernardi. "If anybody remembers selling a bunch of daisies to a man, that's the place we start from. Then we try and find out who he is. Those strands of blond hair from a wig or a toupee may not even be related. For all we know, they're from a bus passenger's doll."

* * *

Samuel took a bus to Sixth and Brennan, the site of the Wholesale Flower Mart. The market was open just three days a week, but Samuel had checked ahead and knew that today was one of those days. He carried a photograph of the daisy found at the crime scene, as well as the police report detailing Grace Conklin's death.

Upon arrival, the aroma of flowers filled his nostrils. Samuel chuckled to himself, noting the irony of finding such delicate, fragrant items in this otherwise downtrodden South of Market Street location, one of San Francisco's roughest areas.

The Wholesale Flower Mart actually housed three distinct markets in separate buildings, each run by a different ethnic group: Italian, Chinese and Japanese. Unsure which to visit first, Samuel headed for the main business office, at 640 Brennan Street. There he inquired about which of the three markets would be most likely to offer daisies. After consulting her chart, the receptionist sent him to the Japanese building.

Walking down the sidewalk towards the double-door entrance of the Japanese market, he again picked up the strong fragrances wafting through the air. When he entered the building he stopped to take in all the colors and scents. It was overwhelming, but in a good way. Once acclimated, Samuel walked down a row of booths until he came to one that sold daisies. There he found daisies of every color imaginable, from bright yellow—like the one he was there to inquire about—to red, purple and even green ones.

A small, bald Japanese man wearing spectacles was stuffing bunches of daisies in flower cones half-filled with water.

Behind a makeshift counter, a Japanese woman wearing an apron over her dress was busy cutting daisies and tying them with string before passing them across to the man.

"Excuse me," said Samuel.

The man looked up. "What can we do for you, young man?" he replied in perfect English.

"Do you sell these flowers to the public as well as to flower stores?"

"Yes, sir. To anyone who has the money to pay for them."

"Are you the only stall in the market that sells daisies?" asked Samuel.

"Yes, sir. The only exception is Mr. Giaconda in the Italian Market, who sells them during the Italian Spring Festival."

"That only happens once a year, correct?"

"Correct."

"I'm a journalist and I'm investigating a murder," said Samuel. "May I show you a photograph?" He pulled the one of the daisy out of his jacket pocket. "This daisy was found at the scene of the crime. You see the sharp angle cut on the stem, and the size? It looks like it could have been one of the oversized ones you sell here."

"That's possible," said the man. "Either it was sold directly by us or we sold it to a flower shop."

"Do you sell small bunches to individuals?" asked Samuel.

"Yes, we sell to all comers," said the man.

"Do you keep track of all your sales?"

"We run a tape every day and we can tell the size of the sale by the amount the customer paid."

"Can you check this date?" Samuel showed him the one on the back of the photograph.

The man handed the photograph to his wife, who wrote the date on a piece of paper and shuffled to the back of the stall, where she rummaged through a drawer. She returned with a piece of adding machine tape clipped to a second piece of paper. The man put the tape on the counter and removed the paperclip, perusing the column of numbers. "According to this," he said, "two different people purchased single bunches of a dozen daisies that day."

Samuel thought for a few seconds. "Do you have any recollection of who those two buyers were?"

"The first purchase in the day was by a customer who buys flowers once a week," the man answered. "She is an old lady in her seventies. I doubt she's a criminal. The other buyer arrived late in the day, almost at closing time. He paid a dollar ninety-eight, which is what we charge for a bunch of daisies. That person could be the one you're looking for."

"Can either of you give me a physical description of this person?"

The couple looked at each other questioningly. After about a minute, the man shook his head apologetically. "I'm sorry, I have no memory of that sale."

"I have a vague recollection," said the old lady, her face brightening. "I remember a man all dressed in black. He had blond hair and was also wearing a black hat. That's why I remember him. It was late in the afternoon and he seemed to be in a hurry. He gave me five dollars and told me to keep the change."

"Did you notice anything unusual about his voice?"

She shook her head.

"How tall was he?" asked Samuel.

"A few inches taller than you but about your build," she answered.

"That's a pretty good day's work." Samuel smiled, amazed he had gotten that much. "Can you remember anything else?"

"Yes," said the woman. "He walked with a limp. There was something wrong with his left leg."

"Like a bad limp or just noticeable?"

"Bad enough for me to notice it."

"Good enough." He took down their names and a phone number, and thanked them. Then he walked to Bernardi's office as fast as his legs would carry him.

* * *

Samuel was still euphoric as he paced the floor of Bernardi's office. "Can you believe our luck?"

"Good day's work, Samuel," said Bernardi with a slight smile. "Now we know we're looking for a man who dresses all in black, wears a blond wig and has or had some kind of a limp."

"Gimme a break," said Samuel. "That's a hell of lot more information than we had this morning. Now we have to figure out who this character is, and whether he had a beef with Jim Abernathy, Chad Conklin or with Grace herself, and whether he's still alive."

"You mean, where did he come from?" asked Bernardi. "My guess is he was a hit man. We have to go out on the street to see if any of our informants can put the finger on him."

"You should widen your net," said Samuel. "I very much doubt the job was given to a local."

"We have ways of sniffing that out," said Bernardi. "I'll put someone on it today."

"Something else bothers me," said Samuel. "What the hell was Grace doing at a bus stop in that neighborhood? I think I'll go and see if I can figure out if there was anything around there that might have interested her. First, though, I'll go back to the medical examiner's and get a photo of her."

"You don't have to go back there," said Bernardi. "I have one." He rummaged through a file on his desk. "Here it is."

"There could be a thousand reasons why she was there that evening," said Samuel, tucking the photo in his pocket.

"Yet there's probably only one right answer."

"You've opened Pandora's box, Samuel. Now pull everything out of it and we'll see if we can connect one thing to another."

"Wait a minute," said Samuel. "Pandora slammed the box shut to prevent despair from coming out. You remember that, don't you?"

"Yes, but I know you, Samuel. You'll find a way to open it again, but without despair interfering."

"You're making a big assumption that I can pull something else out of the box, Bruno."

"I have no doubt," said Bernardi, looking out the window at the cars zooming by on the freeway. "Look what you've done already."

14

Barry Fong-Torres

FOUR PEOPLE WERE GATHERED for tea in the back room of Mr. Song's Many Chinese Herb Shop: Melody, Mr. Song, Samuel and Barry Fong-Torres, who was a new addition to Mr. Song's circle of friends. The terracotta storage jars kept in the front of the shop were visible through the blue beaded curtain that hung in the doorway.

The albino herbalist was dressed in a long black silk robe with embroidered white cranes, one on each side of the front. In contrast to his dark robe and black skullcap, his skin was as pale as ivory. The pendulum of the clock on the wall behind him moved slowly back and forth, reminding Samuel of the gold medallion that Mr. Song had used to hypnotize him to help him stop smoking.

"Mr. Song asked me to introduce the two of you and have you explain why you are here," said Melody.

The newcomer, who was Chinese, put down his teacup and stood to shake Samuel's hand. Samuel guessed he was in his early twenties, though he looked younger. "I'm Barry Fong-Torres," the man said with an engaging smile, his glasses framing intelligent eyes. "Glad to meet you, Mr. Hamilton." He was slightly shorter than Samuel, and his hair was parted on the side, bangs flopping over his forehead.

Melody motioned for them both to sit down. "I know

you're both curious as to why I asked you to come here. Mr. Song would like to meet with both of you about Min Fu-Hok. Mr. Hamilton doesn't speak Chinese, so I'm here to translate for him."

As both men nodded, she reiterated Min Fu-Hok's crimes and the trial's outcome. The light sentence handed down by the judge who tried the case had greatly disturbed Mr. Song, she explained, so he had decided to call for a hearing. He would act as a representative of the people of Chinatown and hear evidence, not just in the case of Mrs. Chow, but also for of all the people who died as a result of drinking the poisoned mineral water.

"I know about the case," said Barry. "It has been the talk of Chinatown, and it was in all the papers."

Mr. Song sipped his tea silently during Melody's introduction. After she finished, he spoke in Cantonese to Barry, with Melody translating for Samuel.

"I know that you are well versed in Chinese history," Mr. Song told Barry, "and you understand what we are about to embark on, don't you?"

"Yes, sir," Barry answered, also in Cantonese.

"I know much about you. I know that you are studying criminology at the University of California in Berkeley. You are also very well connected in Chinatown. I would like you to work with Mr. Hamilton here, who is a trusted friend of mine, to see if the two of you can find out what went on behind the scenes with Mr. Min Fu-Hok."

Barry shook his head. "I'm not sure I follow you. What do you mean, what went on behind the scenes?"

Mr. Song put down the match with which he had just lit an incense stick. "I know that you understand Chinese people, so let me tell you a story. The spirits of those who died as a result of drinking Min's water visited me one night and asked me to pursue justice on their behalf. If they felt justice had been served, they would not have asked me to intervene."

"I understand that you have exceptional powers," answered Barry, "and that you can summon spirits. That's not what's confusing me. I just don't know what you mean by 'behind the scenes.'"

"I want you to investigate this man's background here in Chinatown," said Mr. Song, studying Barry intently, his pale cheeks suddenly flushed. "I want to know how he operated his business, where his money came from for this operation and where it went."

Barry was silent for a moment. "You mean, you want to know if there was anybody else involved in this mess?"

"Yes," said Mr. Song. "Foreign or domestic."

"If there was foreign money involved, how can you do anything about that?"

Samuel saw a hint of a smile appear on Mr. Song's face, something he'd never seen before. "You let me know how can I help," Samuel interjected.

Melody laughed. "I already told you the first time you and I talked. Mr. Song wants you to be a witness to everything that happens. He also wants you to help Barry if he needs it. The only caveat is that you don't disclose what you learn to anyone until you clear it with Mr. Song."

"I need to hear it from him," said Samuel.

The sage nodded.

Samuel knew that was his answer, so he asked Barry if he could talk to him for a few minutes.

"Sure. Let me just clarify our roles." As Barry spoke to Mr. Song again in Cantonese, Melody translated for Samuel: "Melody is going to give me the history of Mr. Min Fu-Hok, and she will explain to me and Mr. Hamilton what you want us to find out about him. You want the information brought to you in a form sufficient for it to be presented to your tribunal. Is that right?"

Mr. Song nodded.

"I need to know a little more about your tribunal," said Barry.

"Melody will explain my tribunal to you. I am the prosecutor and the judge and the finder of the facts. I alone will determine Mr. Min Fu-Hok's guilt and the penalty he has to pay after I review the evidence you bring me and I hear from the witnesses. You and Mr. Hamilton are my investigators. Your job is to find out the things I have asked you about from the Chinese side. Mr. Hamilton will work on the evidence that we can't get through our connections in Chinatown. Is that clear?"

"If I have questions, I will come back and ask you," said Barry.

Mr. Song nodded again and got up and left the room.

* * *

Samuel, Barry and Meloday drank their tea in silence until the incense stick went out. "Do you have any idea where to start?" Samuel asked Barry.

"I have some ideas. But, truthfully, I will have to think about it. Can we get together tomorrow afternoon?"

Samuel nodded and looked at Melody. "I want to help, but right now I can't see how. What is going on here is totally outside my realm of experience. And I'm uncomfortable that I can't share anything I find out with Lieutenant Bernardi."

"But you promised Mr. Song you wouldn't share your findings," Melody reminded him. "Besides, your system has already judged Mr. Min Fu-Hok. There is nothing more they can do to him unless he violates his probation. If, in your investigation, you do find that out that he has, Mr. Song will allow you to turn that evidence over to the authorities. If you discover other things that won't change his status within your justice system, they may still be important for Mr. Song's tribunal. So don't be impatient. You will understand the importance of the evidence when you bring it in and see how Mr. Song uses it."

* * *

After Melody, Barry and Samuel had gone, Mr. Song retired to his private study beside the sitting room where the meeting had been held. The room was lined with floor-to-ceiling bookcases, all crammed with tomes on herbs from around the world. The spines of the books showed every color of the rainbow and their titles were printed in a variety of languages. Cloth bookmarks hung from many of the books, on which a visitor would be hard-pressed to discover a speck of dust.

Mr. Song unbuttoned his black robe, took off his skullcap and sat down at his mahogany desk, which was positioned in the middle of the room. He unrolled the desktop and took out a stick of lemon-scented incense, which he lit. After settling back into his chair, Mr. Song focused his attention on the pendulum of the clock placed on a shelf directly in front of him. The regular movement of the arm soon sent him into the altered state he sought when something was troubling him. He understood that calling for the tribunal was a big responsibility, and he wanted to fulfill his obligation to the community with dignity and efficiency.

During the meeting with Barry and Samuel, Mr. Song had withheld the information that Min Fu-Hok was a client. The Chinese millionaire had paid for two of the large jars prominently displayed in the front of the herb shop. Mr. Song had no idea what was in the jars, but he knew from his careful records that Min Fu-Hok had made several visits to the shop during his criminal case, and had either made deposits or withdrawals from both of them. Looking back now, Mr.

Song guessed that they were probably withdrawals, and the only question was where the money came from. He wanted his investigators to see if they could find that out. Although he also wanted to know where the money went, he knew that that wasn't going to be so easy to find out.

As he went deeper into his trance, Mr. Song visualized a series of Chinatown bank signs, as well as that of the main branch of Bank of America. The images were clear and unequivocal. When they were gone, all he was left with was the silence in the room, the pendulum swinging back and forth and the scent of burning incense.

* * *

Although scheduled to meet Bernardi at Camelot at five-thirty, Samuel arrived an hour early to consult in private with Melba about the meeting at Mr. Song's.

"What exactly does Mr. Song want you to do?" she asked.

"He wants me to gather information from places where his Chinese contacts don't have access."

"For instance?"

"Anywhere that Min Fu-Hok might have bought influence within the halls of power that most Chinese are excluded from, but which Min Fu-Hok might have gotten access to with his money."

"Any ideas about how to go about that?"

"So far the only suggestion I have is from Mr. Song himself. He wants me to get his records from the main office of Bank of America."

"That's a start," she said. "Keep me posted. In the meantime I'll let everything rattle around in my brain."

When Bernardi showed up, he joined Samuel, Melba and Excalibur at the Round Table. Samuel had already given the dog his treat, and Excalibur was wrapped around Melba's chair, asleep. Bernardi sipped a glass of Melba's cheap red wine as Samuel drank his Scotch on the rocks and Melba downed one of several Hamm's beers and chain-smoked her way through a pack of Lucky Strikes.

"I was just at Mr. Song's," said Samuel, careful how he phrased each sentence so as to not reveal to the detective what he'd promised to keep secret. But the truth was that he needed information. "Do you know anything about a Barry Fong-Torres?"

"Yes, we know of him," said Bernardi. "Interesting young man. He is a criminology student at Berkeley. He's in his third year. But he is very active in Chinatown. He knows everybody. We've trying to recruit him for the police department, but he is more interested in the preventative side of the law."

"What does that mean?" asked Samuel.

"He has a big heart and he wants to help those who are already in trouble. The last time I talked to him he was considering working for the probation department. He's particularly interested in helping young people stay away from bad influences."

"Do you trust him?" asked Samuel.

"Absolutely," said Bernardi. "Why do you ask?"

"There is something going on in Chinatown and his name came up," Samuel equivocated. "I'll tell you more when I know something." To change the subject, he queried Bernardi on what was going on with Grace Conklin's case.

"We're running down leads on potential hit men. Right now the description you gave me is circulating in San Francisco, Alameda and Contra Costa."

"Do you think that if someone hired a killer they would stick so close to home?" asked Samuel.

"Never underestimate the arrogance of power," Melba interjected. "People with it are stupid."

Bernardi laughed as Samuel shrugged his shoulders.

15

More Than a Place to Sleep

"I STILL HAVE THAT PHOTOGRAPH of Grace Conklin," Samuel said to Bernardi. "Do you mind if I keep it a little longer?"

"Be my guest."

"I intended to get to this matter sooner, but I got tied up in Chinatown."

"You told me," said Bernardi, shifting the foot-high pile of files on his desk.

Samuel thought—*if he only knew*. He didn't like to keep secrets from Bernardi but he'd given his word to Mr. Song.

"What's your plan?" asked Bernardi, extracting one of the files from the pile.

"I'm not sure I have one," said Samuel. "Ever since this girl was murdered, I've wondered what the hell she was doing in that neighborhood at night. I want to snoop around and see if I can figure it out."

"I wish I could help you, but you can see what I'm up against here," said Bernardi.

"Yeah. I know you're swamped, so I won't waste any more of your time. I'll report in if I get any leads."

* * *

That afternoon, Samuel sat on the same bench that Grace

Conklin had been sitting on the night she was killed. He looked down Harrison Street, quickly deciding it didn't make much sense to head towards the bay; he could see all the way to the Embarcadero, and there wasn't much there to attract anybody's attention. Studying the street in the other direction, he figured he was about six blocks from the Hall of Justice and Bernardi's office. Determining that direction to be his best bet, he gave himself four hours to see if he could find something of interest.

Samuel stopped at several bars along the way, showing Grace's photo to the early-shift employees getting their establishments ready for the evening crowds. Most told him to come back later when the bartender or owner was there. Although Samuel was pretty discouraged by the time he got to Fifth Street, when he saw the Bay Bridge Inn in the middle of the block, it piqued his curiosity, primarily because it was the only building in his way as he walked up the street. Samuel thought he would give the motel a try before getting a bite to eat and then returning to the bars he had visited earlier.

Entering the two-story building's small office, Samuel saw a small, turbaned Indian standing behind the counter. Although young—with an attractive face, black eyes and strong, white teeth—the man looked frail.

"Excuse me sir, can I ask you some questions?" said Samuel.

"Sure boss, go ahead," said the man in broken, accented English.

"I have a photograph of a young woman," said Samuel, pulling the picture of Grace from his jacket pocket. "Have you ever seen her before?"

After studying the photograph a moment, the man looked up at Samuel suspiciously. "Are you police?"

"No, no. I'm a reporter and I'm trying to trace this woman for a story. You know something, don't you?"

"No police?" the man asked again.

"No, I told you, I am a reporter. Tell me what you know."

"Okay, boss. She used to rent a room here. She came once a week for about six months. Then she stopped coming."

"Was it always the same day of the week?"

"Always the same day of the week, on Friday."

"What time would she get here?"

"About four o'clock. When she checked in, she would reserve the room for the next week. Never missed a Friday."

"Was there a particular room she rented?"

"Yes, sir. The last one at the end on the bottom floor, right by the alleyway."

"Did she share the room with anyone?"

"Yes, sir. But I only saw him leave once, when it was already dark."

"Can you tell me what he looked like?"

"No, sir. It was too dark. But I never saw him arrive. She would rent the room and go back there, and he would come in through the alleyway, I guess."

"Can you tell me anything at all about this man?"

"He wore a suit and smoked Parliament cigarettes."

"And that's it?"

"Yes, boss. I just saw his back and it was dark."

"How do you know he smoked Parliament cigarettes?"

"One time I was in there with my cleaning lady. We knew they always left when it got dark, and we wanted to rent the room again because it was Friday night."

"Why do you remember the brand?"

"Because the room smelled like cigarettes and the ashtray by the bed was full, and I looked at the cigarettes."

"You didn't save one by chance?"

"No, boss. Sorry."

"How did they pay for the room?"

"She always paid cash, in advance, on every visit. I never

saw the man."

"Can you tell me anything more about this woman?"

"The last time I saw her leave, she was crying and hitting her hands together."

"You mean, clapping her hands?"

"No, boss, like hitting a closed hand into the other one."

"Like this?" Samuel pounded the fist of his right hand into his left palm.

"Yes, boss, like that."

"Can you tell me when that was?"

The man took the room register out and looked it over carefully, eventually giving the date on which Grace was murdered as the last time he saw her.

"Can I see your register?" asked Samuel.

"I'm not supposed to show this to anybody," said the Indian clerk. "But I let you have peek."

The register was signed Sharon Jones.

"Is this the name she used every time?"

"Yes, boss."

Samuel wrote down the name and the date. "You said she showed up for about six months?"

"Yes, boss."

"Can I have your name?"

"I'll give you my card. You want a room, I'll make special deal for you." The man handed Samuel a card. Below the logo of the Bay Bridge Inn were the words "Rishi Kumar, Manager."

"Do you still have the same cleaning lady that was here when the woman came?"

"Yes, boss."

"What is her name?"

"Magdalena Martinez."

"Does she speak English?"

"*Un poquito*," Rishi answered.

"Do you speak to her in Spanish?"

"*Un poquito,*" he answered, smiling.

Samuel smiled in return, imagining the pair communicating.

"Is she here now?"

"No, it's her day off. She comes back the day after tomorrow."

"What time?"

"She comes at nine in the morning. Works eight hours, but sometimes longer when we are busy."

"Is she the one who always cleaned the room that they always stayed in?"

Rishi thought for a moment. "Yeah, boss. She was the one."

"Can I take a look at the room?"

Rishi nodded, lifting a section of the counter and joining Samuel on the other side. Even with the turban adding to his height, he was still half a head shorter than Samuel. They walked the length of the motel, along the sidewalk. Samuel counted twenty rooms all together, ten on the bottom and ten on top, although just two cars were parked in the lot. When they reached the room nearest the alleyway, Rishi unlocked the door and ushered Samuel inside.

A double bed covered with a faded floral comforter took up most of the space. Nightstands on each side of the bed held plug-in lamps, which were connected to the main light switch. Adjacent to the door was a drop-leaf table flanked by two chairs, and ashtrays littered the room, which reeked of stale cigarette smoke. The cramped bathroom held a commode and a porcelain bathtub with pink tiles lining the walls on three sides; several of the tiles were cracked or missing entirely. A thin towel, more gray than white after too many washings, lay folded over a rack just outside the tub. A plastic shower curtain decorated with pink flamingoes, whose color vaguely matched the tiling, hung from a crooked rod, mold staining the bottom of the curtain where it touched the porcelain.

"They only used this room, correct?" asked Samuel.

"Yes, boss, only this room."

Although Samuel knew he would have to get hold of Bernardi, and that the detective would have Mac go over the room the next day for latent prints and any other evidence, he didn't want to alarm Rishi, who was giving him invaluable information.

"What time do most guests arrive?" asked Samuel.

"Around noon, usually."

Samuel nodded. "Can we take a look at the alley?"

"Sure, boss."

They walked outside and peered up and down the alley, which Samuel calculated was only about ten feet away. Whoever had met Grace was a pretty clever guy, he thought.

"There are plenty of places to park in the alley, I see," he said. "Did you ever see the man park his car in the motel lot?"

"No, boss. If he had, I would have noticed, because all cars have to enter from Harrison Street and leave through the alley."

"Just so I'm sure," said Samuel. "You only saw this man once, from the back, and it was dark and he was wearing a suit, right?"

"Yes, boss."

"Do you know how tall he was?"

Rishi shook his head.

"Can you estimate his weight?"

Samuel got the same answer.

"Can you confirm he was a white man?"

"Only that whoever he was, he wore a suit," said Rishi.

"I'll be back tomorrow with some other people," said Samuel. "In the meantime, don't rent this room to anyone."

Rishi's expression turned suspicious again. "You are police!"

"No, I'm not, I promise. I will keep you out of this but

please don't rent the room." Samuel didn't believe that Rishi knew who had been with Grace during the six months she rented the room, but in case he was wrong, he didn't want to tell Rishi what had happened to her. He didn't want to give the motel manager an opportunity to destroy evidence, if indeed any remained.

"Tell you what I'm going to do," said Samuel. "I will rent the room from you for the night. How much is it?"

"Eighteen seventy-five for one night. You want TV, it's a dollar more."

"No TV, just the room," said Samuel, pulling some bills out of his pocket.

* * *

Bernardi couldn't believe what Samuel had discovered. They went to the evidence locker holding Grace's now-catalogued file and examined each piece of evidence.

"What do you think of those Parliament butts now?" asked Samuel.

"I don't know, frankly. They may have been left there by whoever killed her, by someone who planned it or by a complete stranger."

"You're right," said Samuel. "Without a sample butt from the room to compare these with, we have no way of knowing if the same brand of cigarettes are just a coincidence."

"We may have to wait until the end of this nightmare," said Bernardi. "It could be what holds the case together."

16

Financial Monkey Business

SAMUEL, BARRY AND MELODY huddled over a chow mein bargain lunch at a window table in Chop Suey Louie's, the sweet and sour aromas from the kitchen enveloping them as they discussed Mr. Song's assignment.

"Thanks for explaining how the tribunal works and what Mr. Song is looking for," said Barry. "I was fascinated by the names of some of the banks that Mr. Song saw in his vision. One of them, Bank of America, is not small potatoes. You want me to find out what kind of deposits Min Fu-Hok keeps in them?"

"My uncle is not just interested in what he keeps in them, but also what he withdrew," said Melody. "Mr. Song wants you to find out where the money came from and where it went."

"You know we're going to need some help with this," said Barry.

"Yes, we need a person who understands the Chinese mind and the way it does business," said Melody. "We have to get behind the wall of secrecy that surrounds Chinatown banking."

"What makes you so sure that Min Fu-Hok used banks for his transactions?" asked Samuel.

"Because of Mr. Song's vision and because Min Fu-Hok

had a lot of money at his disposal," said Melody.

"He couldn't keep it all in a place like Mr. Song's, especially after you solved the Chinese Jars murder case," said Barry. "The authorities are wise to that now."

"Where are we going to find a Chinese person who can help us with this?" asked Samuel.

"I have someone in mind," said Barry. "Both of you meet me this evening and we'll pay him a visit."

* * *

At dusk Samuel and Melody met Barry at the corner of Grant Avenue and Jackson Street. They walked down Jackson towards the bay, turning right at Cooper Alley. After a few feet, Barry halted in front of a shabby storefront. "This is it."

"What does it say?" asked Samuel, pointing to the dull-blue Chinese lettering painted on the plate-glass windows.

"Bookkeeping Service," answered Barry.

"Why this place?" asked Samuel.

"Come inside. See for yourself."

The three of them crowded into the cramped entryway, which was set back from the sidewalk. "What does the writing on the door say?" asked Samuel.

"Bookkeeper Jimmy Shu," answered Melody.

She pressed the doorbell, and in no time the door opened and a short bald man wearing a green eyeshade and a faded and smudged green smock stood before them. He backed up to permit them to pass through the small doorway into the office. The light was dim, but it was brighter there than outside. The man smiled, revealing a single tooth hanging from his upper gum, and enthusiastically addressed Barry in Chinese, as if he were an old friend.

"What is he saying?" Samuel asked Melody.

"He's glad to see him and he wants to know how his

family is doing."

"It sounds like he's speaking Cantonese," said Samuel.

"Yes, that's what is spoken in Chinatown," she explained. "The people here are mostly from Southern China."

"Do you know this man too?" asked Samuel.

She nodded. "He has a jar at Mr. Song's."

Once they had all squeezed into the dimly lit office, Samuel looked around, taking in the piles of papers covering the dark-stained wood floor, except for a small space in front of the desk that held a single chair. Some of the stacks were taller than the man himself. Above the desk hung a concave ceiling light, approximately a foot and a half in diameter and open at the top. In the dull light cast by the two low-wattage light bulbs it encased, Samuel could see the carcasses of the dead insects that had accumulated at the bottom of the orb, further impairing the bulbs' already limited ability to light the room.

Samuel took in the surface of the desk as well, observing a green ink blotter and a magnifying glass set atop an inch-thick stack of papers. Next to the stack was a notepad covered in Chinese script, which was illuminated by the reading lamp angled directly over the pile of papers.

Jimmy motioned for them to sit down. Samuel, Barry and Melody looked at each other quizzically, not sure where he meant. After an awkward moment, Melody indicated that Barry should take the only available seat other than Jimmy's, on the far side of the desk.

Jimmy sat down and removed his green eyeshade, exposing his shining bald pate. "What can I do for you, Mr. Fong?" he asked. Melody quietly translated for Samuel.

"We have a request from Mr. Song to get any and all information we can on Min Fu-Hok's assets. Everyone agrees that you are the go-to man when it comes to getting that in Chinatown."

Jimmy, who had been listening intently, nodded his head

in acknowledgment. "This is the man who is the owner of the Flower Blossom Mineral Water Bottling Company?"

"Yes. He's the one we're after."

"First of all, you must understand that my abilities are limited. His transactions have to have left some kind of trail. If I am lucky enough to have picked up something about his accounts on one of my inquiries, I will be able to help you."

"We understand," said Barry, sliding a sheet of paper across the desk to Jimmy. "Here is a list of the banks where Mr. Song thinks he has funds."

Jimmy looked at the names. "I may be able to get information from these three Chinatown banks, but I have no means of acquiring such information on the Bank of America. Sorry."

As Melody finished translating, Samuel raised an eyebrow. "I guess it's up to me to inquire about that one."

"That's why Mr. Song wanted you involved," she said.

"I need a couple of days," said Jimmy. "I have to see what I have in the way of information and I have to make arrangements to get more of it, if needed. Please come back Thursday evening, about this same time."

Both men stood up and Barry reached across the desk and shook hands with Jimmy. The bookkeeper then escorted them to the door and nodded his goodbyes. Once they crossed the threshold, he closed the door and they heard the double click of the deadbolt.

The three walked back in silence to the corner of Jackson Street, where Samuel suddenly halted. "Something is bothering me. Can we hang around for a while and see if he leaves his office? I'd like to know how he gets his information, and something tells me if we follow him, we'll find out."

Barry laughed. "Tell you what, you both go about your business. I'll sit myself down at the counter of that mom-and-pop noodle joint on the corner and see if anything happens at Jimmy's. I have your phone number, Samuel; I'll call you if there's any activity."

"What about me?" asked Melody.

"If you want to be included, give me your phone number as well," said Barry. "I have a feeling it will be a while, so get some sleep."

* * *

It was after midnight when Barry called. Samuel, who had slept with his clothes still on, was back at Barry's side within ten minutes. Melody, who only lived a couple of blocks away, had arrived even sooner. The noodle shop was closed and Barry was standing outside a phone booth, his collar turned up, rubbing his hands together to keep warm. It was one of those typical San Francisco nights—foggy and cold.

"Are you okay?" asked Samuel.

"Yeah," he laughed. "I spent the last hour in the phone booth."

"What's happened here?" asked Samuel.

"Just before I called you, three young men, all dressed in black, went inside Jimmy's. Fortunately for us, they still haven't come out."

Samuel looked at his watch. "That was just a few minutes ago?"

"That's right."

"Is there a rear exit from Jimmy's shop?" asked Samuel.

"There is, but they would still have to come out on Jackson Street. So we're in the right place when they do come out."

They didn't have to wait long. Within a half hour the three young men filed out of the front door of Jimmy's office, each with an empty black sack slung over his shoulder. They separated at the corner of Cooper Alley and Jackson, two heading up the street and the third walking down the hill towards the bay. Samuel indicated that Barry should follow the man going down the street while he and Melody followed the other two up Jackson. Before splitting up, they agreed to meet the next day for lunch at Chop Suey Louie's to report on what they'd found.

When the boys reached Grant Avenue, one turned left. Samuel followed him and Melody tailed the other young man, who continued up Jackson. There were only a few people on the street, so Samuel stayed a safe distance behind his target. He watched him turn the corner at Sacramento Street, where the darkened Bank of Canton sign hung above the double glass doors on Grant Avenue, before continuing up the hill towards the Fairmont Hotel. Once the boy entered the alleyway behind the bank and turned on his flashlight, Samuel ducked into the doorway of a building across the street, where he could watch without been observed. The boy began rummaging through the trash cans, pulling out reams of paper—some crumpled, some not—and examining each batch before stuffing it into his sack. Finally, when the bag was bulging, he turned off his flashlight and threw the sack over his shoulder, retracing his steps all the way back to Jimmy Shu's office.

Samuel went home even more puzzled than he had been before.

* * *

When Samuel walked into Chop Suey Louie's the next day, he found Melody and Barry sitting at the same window table as the day before. Samuel could tell by their faces that they were as confused as he was.

He sat down and poured himself a cup of tea before ordering wonton soup, the special of the day. The other two ordered the soup as well.

"Who goes first?" he asked.

"Melody and I each followed our targets to trash cans located in alleys behind banks," said Barry. "They each rifled through the cans and pulled out papers as if they knew what they were looking for. Once their sacks were full they hauled them back to Jimmy's and that was that."

"I had the same experience," Samuel laughed. "We won't really know what it all means until we have another meeting with Jimmy. But it's hard to imagine that his minions were able to gather specific information about Min Fu-Hok's bank accounts that's going to help us find evidence."

"I don't think that's the point," said Melody. "Let's let him fill us in when we see him next, instead of us groping in the dark trying to figure out the significance of eveything."

"That's Thursday night?" asked Samuel as the soup was brought to the table.

Melody nodded and they all dug in, Samuel savoring the faint smells of sherry and soy sauce as he bit into the chucks of ground pork.

* * *

On Thursday evening Samuel, Barry and Melody once again crammed into Jimmy Shu's packed office. This time Jimmy left his green eyeshade on as he shuffled through the three stacks of papers he had on his ink blotter, one of which was now a foot high.

"Mr. Song called me a couple of weeks ago and asked me to investigate the three banks where you saw my boys go a few nights ago," he said, showing his one-toothed smile. "I've been working on the problem for a while now, but when you came the first time I hadn't put it all together yet. Now I have something for you. These three piles reflect deposits and with-drawals made by Mr. Min Fu-Hok over the last six months. Some of the amounts are very large. You will have to hire an accountant to make any sense of them, but I think you have enough here to keep you busy for some time."

The three investigators looked at each other, amazed to discover how things could be found out in Chinatown. "How much do we owe you for this?" asked Samuel.

Jimmy shook his head. "This is between Mr. Song and me. I will deliver what I have to him this afternoon."

After saying their goodbyes, Samuel, Barry and Melody walked down Cooper Alley. "We still need information from the Bank of America," said Samuel. "Much as I regret having to do this, I'm afraid I'll have to involve my old college buddy Charles Perkins."

"Don't tell Mr. Song," said Melody. "He will not be happy to know that that man is involved in this investigation. Remember he kept Mr. Song's jars when you were working on your first case."

"At some point I'll have to tell him because Perkins is the only person that I know of who can get the information, legally, without getting a warrant. If we discover anything, Mr. Song has to realize that, and he will have to deal with Perkins whether he likes it or not."

"I think he'll let you deal with Perkins," said Melody. "Are we through with our assignment otherwise?"

"We need to have another meeting with Mr. Song after he evaluates what we bring him," said Barry.

"First let me find out if Perkins will help," said Samuel. "If he will, then we make a complete presentation of our findings. Otherwise, we give Mr. Song what we've got and I'll have to figure out a new way to get what we're looking for from the Bank of America."

* * *

Figuring out how to approach Perkins was Samuel's first

order of business. The Assistant U.S. Attorney was still furious with him for having published stories about a Palestinian gunrunner without Perkins' permission; ever since then the attorney had refused to take his phone calls. Samuel felt he was right to go behind Perkins' back, since he'd done all the work to discover the truth about the Palestinian's murder, but that didn't help him at a time like this.

Samuel decided to wait outside the Federal Building with Barry until Perkins left his office for the day, which he usually did around five-thirty. He and Barry got there just before five in case the attorney decided to head out early. When Perkins pushed his way through the main door at five-thirty, Samuel called out to him.

"Charles, we need to talk. I brought a friend who can give you an unbiased account of what we're doing and how you can play an important part in it. You can even get some publicity." He chuckled to himself as he added this last bit, knowing it would get Perkins' attention.

"You're a son of a bitch, Samuel," Perkins retorted. "I'm glad you got fired, you asshole."

"I know you're pissed, Charles, but at least hear us out."

"After what you did to me, never again will I trust you, you greedy bastard." Perkins, who wore his usual faded-blue Cable Car three-piece suit, was red-faced and sputtering. "You think only of yourself, and never of your friends."

Samuel knew better than to try and argue. At the same time, he knew Perkins was still talking to him because he could never pass up an opportunity for publicity.

"Just hear us out," Samuel implored.

"You don't understand. I gave you an order. I brought you the people who made your case and the only single thing I asked of you was that you wait until I gave you permission to disclose what you learned from them. But, no, you and your fucking ego had to blab it all over the press that Israel had the bomb. You shithead! I swore I was never going to talk to you again."

Even as spoke, however, Samuel could see by his expression that he was curious to hear more.

"What do you want now, anyway?" asked Perkins

"Barry can tell you better than I can," said Samuel. He'd already told Barry not to mention Mr. Song, and to instead just let Perkins know that the evidence was mounting that Min Fu-Hok was up to his neck in potentially illegal activity that might entail a federal crime. Following Samuel's instructions, Barry explained that they needed access to Min Fu-Hok's accounts at the Bank of America to see if he had hidden any illegal money there.

"What do you mean, illegal money?" asked Perkins with new interest.

"We mean that he apparently got his hands on a lot of money illegally imported from the Far East, but we can't trace the sources right now," said Barry. "We need your help to find out where it's coming from. I can tell you one thing, though, it's a lot."

"What do you mean, a lot?" asked Perkins.

"Millions," said Barry.

Perkins's eyes widened and Samuel knew they had him. This was the kind of game Perkins liked to play.

"What's in it for me?" the attorney demanded.

"You get to expose a criminal who managed to evade the San Francisco judicial system in the first go around," said Barry.

Perkins didn't say anything, but Samuel could tell he liked the idea.

"Come to my office tomorrow at ten, and I'll see what I can do." Perkins turned abruptly, without saying goodbye, and headed up Seventh Street toward Market.

Samuel and Barry stayed put. They looked at each other

and smiled. "Thanks for helping me with him," said Samuel. "You said all the right things. He was so pissed at me that if I were the one to make the request, he might not have budged."

"You must know him pretty well," said Barry.

"Very well," said Samuel. "Buy you dinner?"

"I'll flip you for it," answered Barry, knowing that either way they would go to Chinatown.

* * *

The next morning Samuel and Barry sat for ten minutes in the sitting room outside Perkins' office before being ushered in. Once inside, Samuel saw that things hadn't changed much since his last visit. Boxes of closed cases were stacked against the walls, and Perkins' desk was as cluttered with papers as ever, with only a narrow space carved out of the middle where he could stretch his legs while reading the morning paper. He was wearing the same faded blue suit of the previous day, but he'd spruced up his outfit with a light yellow shirt and bright red tie.

Setting down his cup of coffee, Perkins motioned for his guests to sit in the two seats opposite his desk. "I've decided to help you with this investigation," he said. "But before I do that, in light of our previous misunderstanding, I've prepared a short contract for you to sign." He handed each of them a fifteen-page, single-spaced document.

Samuel skimmed the agreement. "Wait a minute!" he said, appalled by what he'd read. "You're a public official. I'm bringing you a complaint and giving you an opportunity to investigate it, and maybe even get another conviction, and you treat Barry and me like we're the criminals here. What the hell's wrong with you?"

Perkins' face flushed and he crossed his arms defiantly.

"Do you want my help or not?"

"That depends on what price we have to pay to get it."

"Sign the goddamned contract."

"Not a fucking chance," barked Samuel, getting up to leave. "Come on, Barry, let's get the hell out of here."

As Samuel and Barry reached the door, Perkins stood up. "Hold on—come back and sit down," he said, wiping his sweaty hands on his shiny suit pants. "I'll help you. Tell me what you've got so far."

* * *

That evening after work, Samuel went to Camelot to see Blanche and have a drink with Melba. Blanche wasn't in yet, so he sat down with Melba, who was smoking a cigarette and having a beer at the Round Table. "You look down," said Samuel. "What's wrong?"

"I could tell you it was that time of the month, but I'm way past that stuff." She laughed, but Samuel picked up a note of sadness.

"No, really," said Samuel as Excalibur nuzzled up to him, searching for his habitual treat. "What is it?"

"I just lost two sisters who were good pals of mine."

"You mean they both died?"

"Yep, the big C got them. And they were younger than me."

"You never know for whom the bell tolls," said Samuel.

"Yeah," she said, smiling wanly. "I'm amazed it hasn't rung for me yet."

"You're depressed," said Samuel. "Is there anything I can do for you?"

"Nah. You know the drill. Just have to grit my teeth and get over it."

Samuel nodded sympathetically, scratching the earless

side of Excalibur's head.

"Distract me," she said. "Tell me what's happening in your world."

"It's complicated. I actually have a lot to tell you. But you understand that what I'm about to confide can't leave the room? It's very sensitive stuff."

Melba raised her chin indignantly. "Have I ever...?" she started, her face reddening.

Samuel lifted his hand as if to ward off a storm. "Sorry, I know better than that. It's just that I spent a grueling morning with Charles Perkins. He put me through the wringer before agreeing to help." He then proceeded to explain what was going on at Mr. Song's and what they'd uncovered about the Chinese millionaire's holdings and some of his hidden assets.

"The problem is that we know he has money hidden somewhere," Samuel concluded, "but we don't know where to look."

Just then, Blanche walked in through the back door and gave them a whistle and a wave. Her cheeks were bright pink, as if she'd been running. Samuel jumped up. "I'll be right back, Melba." He walked quickly to the back of the bar and embraced Blanche, wrapping his arms around her.

"Hi, handsome," she said, kissing him firmly on the mouth. "Have you missed me? I haven't seen you for more than a week."

"You're warm. Did you run here from home?"

"Sure did. It only took me forty minutes."

Samuel held her out in front of him and looked at her admiringly. Her white sweats were damp with perspiration, but even so, she had a sweet aroma, he thought. "Can we get together after work tonight?"

"Tomorrow is better. It's my day off. We can cook some vegetarian food at your apartment and go to the movies. What do you say?"

"Sounds good to me. What time?"

"I'll come over at six and we can go shopping down on Stockton Street, okay?"

Samuel nodded and she turned to look out over the bar. "I see we have a thirsty crowd here. I'd better get to work. You talked to Mom? She's got the blues."

"I picked that up. I've tried to distract her with my intrigues. Let's see if that helps."

"See you tomorrow, handsome. Don't get home late and leave me sitting on the stairs." She kissed him, gently this time, and he wandered back to the Round Table.

Samuel was surprised to find that Melba's mood had changed; she was suddenly animated. "I've been thinking," she said, smiling as she flicked the ash from her cigarette into an ashtray. "I have a lead for you to follow."

"That was fast. What is it?"

"Find out what Min Fu-Hok's wife does in her spare time."

17

What a Pimp Can Tell You

THIS WASN'T MY IDEA, Samuel thought as he rode the F train to the East Bay, but he had to admit that it was creative, and he had to follow all leads.

After exiting in Emeryville, he took an AC Transit bus to San Pablo Avenue and made his way to the address Bernardi had given him, climbing the rickety stairs of the Victorian house. It had once been a working stiff's pride and joy but now, its paint peeling, it was just another ramshackle house in a decaying neighborhood as the Negro population of West Oakland crept towards Oakland's downtown.

He knocked on the door. There was no response. He knocked again, this time harder. It wasn't until his third try that he saw a small black hand push aside the soiled lace curtain covering a small window in the center of the door. After a moment, the front door slowly opened and a slender Negro girl of perhaps twenty stood in front of him. She had on a red T-shirt and Levis, and wore black Capezios on her feet.

"Yes sir," she greeted him. "What you want?"

"I came to see George."

"Hold on," she said, slamming the door shut.

As Samuel stood on the porch, watching people go by, he realized that he was the only white person on the block.

After a few minutes, the girl opened the door again. "What you want?"

"Bernardi sent me."

She moved to close the door again but Samuel jammed his foot into the opening to stop her. "Look, if I have to wait, I'd rather do it inside."

"Alright," she conceded grudgingly. "Go in there." She pointed to a sitting room off the entry hall. Samuel complied, and after a quick look out the dirty bay windows—covered by the same lace curtains as the window in the door, though these hadn't seen as much traffic—he sat down on the tattered blue velvet sofa to peruse the well-thumbed magazines on the coffee table. It was a choice between editions of *Life* or *Ebony*, both from years past. He picked up *Life*, which was dated November 9, 1959, and featured a photograph of Marilyn Monroe on the cover. She wore a black dress and was jumping in the air, her feet tucked beneath her. Her back was to the camera, but she'd turned to smile over one shoulder. Samuel thought back to her death the year before, the probable result of suicide. He made himself comfortable on the sofa and leafed through the pages, admiring the new-model 1960 automobiles on display.

As he waited, alone, several young women with varying skin tones walked by the sitting room to peek at him. After a half hour, when he was just about to get up and leave, a tall Negro man with an ugly scar on his cheek entered the room. He wore a black suit, a green silk shirt, crocodile cowboy boots and the largest gold medallion Samuel had ever seen hanging from anyone's neck. Samuel was sure that the black suit, not to mention the scar, was intended to make the man look menacing, and it worked. He was no one you would want to meet anywhere alone, day or night.

"I'm George," the man said by way of greeting. "What Bernardi want?"

"I'm sure it's more of the same," said Samuel, standing up

to introduce himself and shake the man's large hand. "We're trying to find a man about my height"—Samuel based his estimation on what he had learned from the Japanese couple at the flower mart—"and he has or had a limp."

"That's all you got, Mister?"

"We know he was dressed in black and wearing a blond wig."

George smiled. "Looky here. There's dudes that use my girls and sometimes they come dressed up in all kinds of funny costumes. I'm not sure why, 'cause you can spot 'em from a mile away. The blond hair and the black duds don't mean shit. But the limp ain't something that someone usually can fake, and it may register with me."

Just then, a pretty young Negro girl walked into the room holding a wire coat hanger. Tears ran down her cheeks. Her hair, straight except for the roots, which were frizzy, was a mess. "I been thinkin'," she said. "You right, George. I need some ass kickin'." She handed him the hanger.

He looked at her in silence for a few seconds. "Awright. You go to your room. I'll be there as soon as I finish my business here."

She turned and left. George remained standing in the middle of the room, toying with the piece of wire and gently whacking it against his palm. Samuel watched, wondering what was going on, but sure he shouldn't ask.

"These goddamned broads," George said. "Sometimes they get out of line, and I has to discipline 'em. They always overreact, but when they settle down, they come back and ask for the punishment."

"Are they all young like her?" asked Samuel.

"Not all, but more than you would think. Maybe they didn't get enough parenting when they was real young." He laughed. "So they come to daddy to get what they think they deserve."

Samuel shook his head. "I can only imagine."

"Let's get back to our business. Bernardi know I don't work for free, and now you know that, too."

"Yeah. He told me he'd make good on any information you have for us."

"Okay," said George, settling into an oversized armchair next to the sofa. "Sit back down, Mr. Samuel. Let me go over this here thing in my head." Samuel nodded and waited.

"The limp's the thing that comes back to me," said George after a few minutes. "I knows a guy that likes my chicks a lot. On occasion he's roughed a couple of 'em up, and I had to have a little talk with him. He's the only one I can think of that fits your description. He's from around here, and he's done some bad shit. He's like a gun for hire, and he's even done some time when he stepped over the line and got caught."

"Do you know if he's ever killed anyone?"

"I ain't saying that. I knows he's beat the shit out of few people who didn't pay their bills on time, and I tol' you, he's roughed up a couple of my girls."

"Who is he, and where can I find him?"

"Not so fast...Mr. Samuel, I needs for Bernardi to give me a visit, and I needs to see some 'do re mi.'" He chuckled. "I'm telling you this much so you can report back to him that George may have a live one for him. So when he come back with a hundred bucks, we can talk business."

"Can't I bring you the money and get the information?"

"No, siree. I likes to look Bernardi in the eye when I let go of information, and I likes him to pay me personally. That way I knows he's going to keep it just between us boys."

"Won't the girl who answered the door remember that I told her Bernardi sent me?"

"She don't know Bernardi from the man in the moon, and I don't even have to tell her you were never here." He stood up. "Now, unless you're interested in one of my young ladies, I got some chores to look after…"

"I don't think so, not today," said Samuel. "Thanks anyway. Bernardi will be in touch pretty quick. He'll be happy to know you have a possibility for him."

18

Conklin Pays the Piper

THE DISTRICT ATTORNEY'S OFFICE was busy preparing its case against Conklin. The Grand Jury had returned its indictment against him for voluntary manslaughter in the death of Carlos Sanchez, for intentionally hiding a material witness to a crime, and for interfering with a police investigation.

When Conklin, accompanied by his three attorneys, made his court appearance to enter a plea, Samuel was in the courtroom, and he made sure Conklin saw his smiling face. After being fired for writing in his story that Conklin had hidden a witness—which Conklin had claimed was libelous—this was a major vindication for Samuel. Although Samuel had personally found the witness, he wasn't at all surprised that Conklin pleaded not guilty. The defendant knew the evidence against him was overwhelming and was stalling for time so he could work out a plea for a reduced sentence.

During the hearing, Samuel relived some of the horrible images of that tragic day. He remembered Carlos' body lying on the ground, covered with muck, and the graphic descriptions Sambaguita Poliscarpio had given in his statement about how terrifying it had been to be stuck in the muck at the bottom of the tank, breathing in the toxic fumes because their face masks didn't work.

Samuel was happy for the Sanchez family, since they had suffered the brunt of the tragedy and the unfairness of the delay. He'd made sure they were well-represented by sending them to his attorney friend Janak Marachak, who'd represented others afflicted by ruthless companies' careless and sometimes reckless use of chemicals. After the court hearing, Samuel called Janak to tell him what had happened at the courthouse.

"Conklin has entered a plea of not guilty and is going to go to trial on all the charges. It's all going to happen pretty fast now."

"I'm glad to hear that," said Janak. "Did you know that I settled the case against some of the peripheral defendants, so that Carlos' family and even Roberto have been partially compensated for the shit that Conklin is responsible for."

"That's good to know," said Samuel. "Who's left in the case?"

"Conklin Chemical and Conklin himself. They can be sued under the labor code, even though workers' compensation is the sole remedy under California law for injured workers."

"How does that work?" asked Samuel.

"There's an exception," Janak explained. "If the employer intentionally causes an injury to a worker, he can be sued. The problem with all this is that if Conklin Chemical or Conklin himself is found to be responsible for Carlos' death or Roberto's injuries, there's no insurance coverage. But because there has been a delay, I haven't been able to find out what Conklin's assets are or where he keeps them."

"Why not?"

"Since he's been under suspicion of a crime, I can't get any information about him or anything he owns," Janak answered. "He has the law on his side. I wouldn't be able to find that out anyway without first getting a judgment against him. I'm sure he's gotten rid of most of his assets by now. On the other hand, there is the legal doctrine that says you can't defraud creditors. If we can show that he intentionally did get rid of assets while this case was pending, we can go after them."

"That may not be so easy. We may never know what he owns or where he has it hidden," said Samuel. "We're not dealing with Mr. Nice Guy here."

"Can't help it. We'll just have to wait until we get a judgment against him and then clean up the mess."

* * *

In the end, however, the Sanchez family didn't have to wait long for closure. Within two days of his meeting with Janak, Samuel got a call, after midnight, from one of his sources, and rushed to the scene of an accident on the Bay Bridge.

The next day he got a headline and byline in the afternoon paper:

Chemical Exec Killed in Fiery Crash

Chad Conklin, a well-known East Bay chemical executive, who was awaiting trial on manslaughter charges in the death of one of his workers, burned to death early this morning when his Mercedes Benz sports car plowed into a Bay Bridge tow truck that had stopped behind a disabled vehicle. No one else was injured in the crash. The California Highway Patrol indicates that the apparent cause of the accident was brake failure.

First thing that morning, even before the paper had gone to press, Janak received a call from Samuel, informing him that Conklin had been killed in the accident and that the California Highway Patrol and SFPD were conducting an investigation to determine if there had been any foul play.

When Janak hung up the phone, he didn't waste any time.

"You'd better get Roberto Sanchez in here quick," he told his secretary, Marisol Leiva, who was also Bernardi's girlfriend. Because of that fact, Janak reminded her that anything that went on in his law office was nobody else's business.

The next day, Roberto was waiting for Janak when he arrived at his office, which was located on the third floor of a small building overlooking a Chinese restaurant. The young man had never regained the weight he'd lost after his accident at Conklin Chemical, and he still had breathing problems, but he'd managed well enough to be working again. Roberto greeted Janak with a wheeze but was otherwise in good spirits. The two men shook hands.

"How are you feeling these days?" asked Janak.

"I get along. Ever since I got away from the chemical plant, things are much better,"

"Listen, I have some bad news to tell you. Chad Conklin, the owner of the chemical company where you were injured, was killed a couple of nights ago. That is not good for our case. I tried to get in touch with your cousin's wife, but the phone number I have isn't any good. Did she move?"

"She is visiting one of our uncles in Mexico City," Roberto answered. "She be back home next week. She cut the phone off to save money. But I already told her about Mr. Conklin dying," he added, adjusting himself in the chair positioned in front of Janak's desk. He sat erect but seemed relaxed.

"So you knew about this?" asked Janak, surprised.

"*Sí señor,* my boss showed me the paper and explained it to me at the place where I work."

"Where do you work now, Roberto?"

"At the Mercedes Benz dealership in Oakland."

"Where?" Janak looked startled.

"At the Mercedes dealership," repeated Roberto, looking Janak in the eye.

"Isn't that where Chad Conklin had his car repaired?"

asked Janak, giving him a searching look.

"So they say."

Janak looked out the window toward Second Street, slowly twisting a pencil between his fingers. After a long silence he turned to Roberto. "It's probably time for you to go back to Mexico."

"*Sí, señor.* It is time for me to go home."

Roberto and Janak stood up. They said their goodbyes, and as Roberto was getting ready to leave, Janak smiled. "Strange the way things happen sometimes."

"*Sí, señor.* Sometimes very unexpected things happen."

*   *   *

At about the time Roberto was leaving Janak's office, Samuel and Bernardi were in the detective's office going over what they knew. "The mechanics in our forensic unit have gone over what's left of the car," said Bernardi, "and it looks like the brakes failed."

"You mean someone tampered with them?"

"They can't say that for sure, but they showed me a loose hydraulic line," said Bernardi. "It wasn't cut or anything, but it had come loose and was dangling. And there was no brake fluid left in the brake system."

"Could they get any prints off it?"

"It was too burned," said Bernardi. "We found out where Conklin had his car serviced, and subsequently called the Mercedes Benz dealership in Oakland to get a look at their repair records. Look at this." Bernardi showed Samuel the invoice. "It shows that a few days ago Conklin took his car there for a routine, ten-thousand-mile check up. Now, look at the items checked off as completed. There's a check mark next to 'brakes.'"

"Did you ask them what was usually done?"

"Yes," said Bernardi. "All the connections are checked and they're supposed to make sure the hydraulic fluid level is up to snuff. See"—he pointed—"here it is marked 'okay.'"

"Did you find out who the mechanic was who worked on it?"

"Yes," said Bernardi, "but that's not what's important. Look here, look who signed the take-in for the car. It was Roberto Sanchez."

"Wait a minute," said Samuel, wide-eyed. "Is that the same Roberto Sanchez who used to work for Conklin? I can't believe it."

"We don't know that for a fact. We do know, however, that Sanchez no longer works for Conklin Chemical."

"What about the dealership? Have you asked them if they know?"

"We asked them if Sanchez used to work for Conklin Chemical and they told us that he did. So we told them we wanted to interview this Roberto Sanchez. They told us that he hasn't shown up for work the past few days."

"Was he the mechanic who worked on the car?"

"No way. He'd have to be German to work on a Mercedes. But I bet he was around it enough to cause some damage if he wanted to."

"Sounds like we have to pay Janak a visit then, doesn't it?" said Samuel.

*　*　*

The next morning saw Samuel and Bernardi at Janak's new offices, where he'd relocated earlier that year. The elevator opened directly onto the reception area. Marisol, Bernardi's girlfriend, greeted them politely; on this day she was wearing another hat—that of Marachak's secretary.

"Gentlemen," she said, her smile professional. "Mr.

Marachak is expecting you." She no doubt had already told him they would be in that morning. "Go right in."

Bernardi instantly took charge of the meeting. "Hello, Mr. Marachak. Long time no see."

"Nice to see you, Lieutenant. How are things?"

"I've had better days," answered Bernardi.

"Thanks for the information about Conklin the other day, Samuel," Janak said. "I appreciate it."

"That's actually why we're here," said Bernardi. "We're looking for your client, Mr. Roberto Sanchez."

"Yes, I understood that from Samuel's call yesterday. Come into my office and sit down. Want a cup of coffee?"

"No thanks," they answered, taking their seats as Janak closed the door to his spacious office, which was located in the far corner of the third-floor space. Gold block letters announcing his law practice filled the large plate-glass window.

Janak listened stone-faced to Bernardi's inquiries about Roberto Sanchez, rolling the pencil he was holding between his thumb and forefinger. The detective outlined what they had learned from the Highway Patrol investigators and from his own forensic staff, and explained that it was necessary to interview Roberto. When he finished, there was silence.

"I can't help you much with Mr. Sanchez," Janak finally said. "Anything I know about him or his whereabouts is confidential. It's all protected by the attorney-client privilege. So my lips are sealed."

"You understand this is a homicide investigation?"

"It doesn't matter what kind of an investigation it is. I can't divulge any information about my client to you or anybody else under any circumstances without his permission."

"Well, get it," insisted Bernardi.

Samuel smiled; he knew better. Janak shook his head. "Not a chance in hell."

"Then we'll have to subpoena you before the Grand Jury,"

said Bernardi, now red-faced and shaking with anger.

"It doesn't matter," said Janak. "The conversation about my client is over for now. In any case, there have to be other possibilities here, don't you think? His wife was murdered by a person or persons unknown, and maybe there is a connection between what happened to her and what just happened to him."

"That may be," said Bernardi, "and we'll explore all those possibilities, but as a cop I have to start someplace, and your client working at the shop that did the repairs on the victim's car is my first stop, with or without your help."

"It will definitely be without my help," Janak said. He stood, grim-faced, and bade his visitors goodbye.

19

Justice in Chinatown

THE CHINESE COMMUNITY's most distinguished elders were crowded in rows of folding chairs in the back room of Mr. Song's Many Chinese Herb shop. Mr. Song was dressed in a plain black silk robe and a black silk skullcap. As usual, his outfit contrasted with his pale white skin and red eyes, which were magnified by his glasses, giving him the appearance of a supernatural being.

He sat behind a table, which was also covered in black silk and was elevated on a platform. At another table in front of the platform sat Min Fu-Hok, who had been kidnapped and was being held at a secret location. Two Chinese businessmen dressed in expensive Western suits sat at his table, acting as his counsel. At a third table sat three elders wearing traditional Chinese robes, along with Barry Fong-Torres, who had assumed the role of chief investigator for Mr. Song's tribunal.

Samuel and Melody sat in the back row. The room overflowed with the citizens of Chinatown, including the loved ones of the twenty-two victims whose families claimed they'd died after drinking poisoned water from the Flower Blossom Mineral Water Bottling Company.

Mr. Song raised his hand and the buzzing crowd fell silent. He surveyed them, took a deep breath and began to speak,

Melody translating for Samuel. Mr. Song said that Min Fu-Hok had been called before him to answer for crimes against the people of Chinatown that hadn't been addressed in the American system of justice. Therefore, it was the tribunal's responsibility to examine what he had done and to render an appropriate judgment—guilty or not guilty. He wanted it understood that Min Fu-Hok was there involuntarily, and if he tried to flee he would be forcibly returned to hear the evidence and the tribunal's sentence.

"Mr. Min Fu-Hok, now I'm going to explain to you why this tribunal was necessary. You were tried under the American system of justice for the death of one person, but from the evidence we have gathered and which will be available to you to examine, and rebut if you can, a total of twenty-two persons died as a result of your conduct. You need to answer for those deaths. Do you have any questions before we start?"

Min Fu-Hok stood and addressed Mr. Song. "To you, most honorable judge of this, what you call a tribunal, this is the United States of America. When you and the others in this room who are accusing me of the deaths of all these people became residents or citizens of this great country, you swore that you would submit to its laws. I have already been judged by the laws of this state. I have been sentenced and have agreed to pay a fine. That is my punishment. What you are doing is extrajudicial and is, frankly, against the laws you agreed to live by."

Samuel laughed when he heard Min Fu-Hok's response. "According to Samuel Johnson, patriotism is the last resort of a scoundrel," he whispered to Melody.

Mr. Song studied Min Fu-Hok, his expression neutral. "This tribunal will determine if you have lived by those laws or attempted to subvert them by illegal means. If I find that you have lived by them, you will go free.

"First, we will deal with the evidence. Mr. Fong-Torres, I

asked you to collect the death certificates of the twenty-two dead. You did that for me, didn't you?"

"Yes, Mr. Song, I did, and I have provided them to you."

"Except for that of Mrs. Chow, each of them indicates that the person died of natural causes. Is that correct?"

"Yes, Mr. Song."

"I also asked you to have hair samples of those twenty-one people chemically tested, did I not?"

"Yes, Mr. Song. The families all clipped locks of hair from their relatives as keepsakes before their cremations. And the hair samples of all twenty-one were laced with arsenic, as was the water from the Flower Blossom Mineral Water Bottling Company."

"You may have copies of all these tests, if you desire them," Mr. Song told Min Fu-Hok, who declined to answer. His advisers also remained silent, and the envelope lay unopened on their table.

"Do you wish to contest the finding of the pathology report on the twenty-two dead?" asked Mr. Song.

"Mr. Fong-Torres, did you at my request get affidavits from members of the twenty-one families swearing that each decedent has drunk Flower Blossom Mineral water on many occasions before their deaths?"

"Yes, Mr. Song, here they all are alphabetized by last name," said the investigator.

"Did you make an extra copy of the affidavits?" asked the judge.

"Yes, I did."

"Will you please pass those copies to Mr. Min."

"I contest everything that goes on in this tribunal," said Min Fu-Hok, his face red.

"Your words are not enough," said Mr. Song, removing his thick glasses. "Do you wish to submit competent proof of your position?"

Min Fu-Hok made no reply, and Mr. Song waited for a full minute before proceeding. He put his glasses back on and looked down at the next page of Chinese script in front of him. "Very well. Next we move to the financial aspect of your case. At the request of my investigator, the bookkeeper Mr. Jimmy Shu looked into your accounts at several Chinatown banks. He found deposits from a numbered Swiss bank account just before your trial started. Will you tell this tribunal what the purpose of those deposits was?"

Min Fu-Hok stood up, his face now an even deeper shade of red. "I will not lower myself to disclose my financial dealings with this tribunal. There is absolutely no proof that any of those transactions had anything to do with the cases of these dead people in Chinatown. Besides, you were never given permission to look into any of my financial transactions or holdings. I can report you to the police for that. That is against the law of this state."

"You know too much about the law of this state and not enough about your obligations to the citizens of Chinatown," responded Mr. Song. "If you do not tell us the nature of those transactions and for whom they were intended, we will presume they were made either to hide money in case you were convicted or for some other criminal venture. Your silence goes against your interests."

"I have nothing more to say to you, old man," said Min Fu-Hok. "You are violating my rights as a citizen. I will turn this matter over to the District Attorney and have my lawyers sue you."

An irritable rumble arose from the crowd. Samuel, who was busy taking notes for his stories, leaned over and whispered to Melody, "Is it a good idea for him to be attacking Mr. Song in this forum?"

"Not a good idea," said Melody.

"But Mr. Song seems to be above his insults," said Samuel.

"I get the feeling that he is on another plane, and that the people are with him. It's as if the crowd has surrendered to his vision and they feel he will give them justice—the justice that was denied to them in the American system."

When the crowd had calmed down, Mr. Song said, "There is another issue this tribunal needs to inquire about. Your wife has a fabric and doll shop, which is apparently very successful. We understand that in the basement of the shop you store a lot of gold. Is that true?"

This was news to Samuel. He remembered that Melba had questioned him as to what Min Fu-Hok's wife did. He poked Melody, asking for more information. She put her finger to her lips. "Shhh. I'll fill you in later."

"How dare you bring my wife into this," said Min Fu-Huk, visibly angry. "She has done nothing wrong and your accusations against her are defamatory."

"You must listen to my question, Min Fu-Hok," responded Mr. Song. "I am not accusing your wife of anything. I am asking you if you have gold hidden in the basement of her shop."

"I don't have to answer that."

Mr. Song raised an eyebrow. "We are trying to determine if any of that gold was used to influence the result you obtained in your criminal trial. Do you wish to answer that question? You must have records of the amounts of gold you disposed of before and during your trial. We would like to see your accounting."

Min Fu-Hok again stood and huddled with his two representatives. After a lengthy and hushed discussion, he again addressed the tribunal. "I do not acknowledge your claim that I have gold underneath my wife's shop. I can't show you any accounting of something that does not exist." He sat back down.

"Mr. Fong-Torres, do you have an affidavit in your pile of

evidence that contradicts what this man is saying?" asked Mr. Song.

"Yes, Mr. Song. We have an affidavit from one of his former employees, a Mrs. Wuan, who states that there is a cellar under his wife's shop that holds a vault. She attaches a ledger sheet that shows the amounts that have been withdrawn, as well as the dates. They correspond to the time he was on trial for manslaughter. She is now in hiding and under your protection so that no harm comes to her."

"Will you please give Min Fu-Hok a copy of the affidavit?" said Mr. Song. "Also attached to the affidavit is copy of a deposit slip that shows that a quantity of gold was transferred to the same Swiss bank account where you deposited money from some of the Chinese banks. Do you deny that that transaction took place?"

Instead of answering him, Min Fu-Hok rose in defiance. "I challenge the legitimacy of this tribunal. You have invaded my privacy and stolen my property. I am leaving this place and I am going to report you to the authorities."

With that he and his companions got up to leave, but five men quickly filled the aisle and blocked their progress by forming a wall, two in front and three behind, all with their arms folded. Min Fu-Hok screamed, "You can't do this to me!" The two men in front spun him around to face the dais where Mr. Song was still seated, calmly observing the fracas.

"When you are ready we will proceed with the hearing," said Mr. Song. The crowd clapped. This was their day in court, and Mr. Song was socking it to Min Fu-Hok. The two men marched the prisoner back down the aisle to his seat. Min Fu-Hok's representatives had already returned to their table; they knew better than to get in the way.

Samuel wrote furiously in his notebook. "Where did he get all this information?" he asked Melody. "I knew about the Chinese bank accounts, but this is much more damaging."

Melody again put her finger to her lips. "I'll tell you all about it after the hearing."

* * *

Mr. Song raised his hand and the crowd quieted. He turned to Min Fu-Hok. "Is there something you'd like to say to this tribunal or to the families that have accused you of causing the death of their loved ones?"

Min Fu-Hok, now grim-faced, said nothing.

"I will take your silence as a 'no,' " said Mr. Song. "The tribunal has studied the evidence carefully. It includes a study of the bottled water from the Flower Blossom Mineral Water Bottling Company, not only in the bottles but also in the tanks at your factory. Both contained high percentages of arsenic, a poison. We also traced that water from its source in the Fort Ross State Park, and found that it contains the highest concentration of arsenic of any water source in the State of California.

"We also learned from your employees that they were sworn to secrecy about how they processed the water at your plant. Moreover, we know that there was no process by which the water was tested or treated for the high degree of arsenic it contained, and that you made no attempt to filter it before it was bottled." Mr. Song glanced around the room, taking in his rapt audience.

"In addition, the locks of hair taken from the twenty-one people who died and were subsequently cremated showed they had enough arsenic in their systems to kill them. Therefore, we made the connection that the arsenic in the bottled water did just that. We have excluded the death of Mrs. Chow from this trial because you have already been tried and convicted for that crime.

"The tribunal finds that you are responsible for taking the

lives of the other twenty-one people. That is my judgment. Tomorrow I will pronounce sentence on you. Until then, you will remain under the control of the tribunal at a secret location known only to me and to the guards I have appointed to watch over you. Any attempt on your part to escape, or by any of your agents to set you free, will be dealt with sternly and could result in death. Do you understand that? More important, do your representatives understand that?"

Min Fu-Hok and his counselors nodded grimly.

Mr. Song removed his glasses and cleaned them with a white silk cloth he pulled from his jacket pocket. When he was done, he put them back on. "In keeping with tradition," he continued, "you are entitled to eat anything you like this evening before your sentence is pronounced tomorrow."

After a brief consultation, one of Min Fu-Hok's representatives stood to address Mr. Song. "Mr. Min Fu-Hok desires Mongolian beef, pork fried rice and two bottles of tiger bone wine for his meal with us this evening."

"Very well," said Mr. Song. "His request will be honored. And now, the open session of this tribunal is concluded. Tomorrow I will announce Min Fu-Hok's sentence in private. No one from the public will be allowed." With that, Mr. Song left the dais.

Samuel looked out at the crowd, which had lingered to discuss the proceedings. "Folks looked pretty satisfied," he said to Melody. "What do you think the sentence will be?"

"Only Mr. Song knows that," she answered.

"Well, I can't wait to find out so I can complete my story."

Melody frowned. "I doubt if anyone will ever know."

"You've got to be kidding," said Samuel. "The public will read this incredible story and not find out how it ends?"

"I think the families who have been harmed by him know what the end will be," said Melody.

"And that is?"

"Ask them. I can't tell you."

"You mean, you won't tell me," said Samuel.

"That's right," answered Melody.

"Pretty unfair and very disturbing, Melody. It's public knowledge that I helped with the investigation, and now I won't be able to do anything more than guess what the outcome will be. Right now, my sense is that it's going to be 'sinister,' to use one of Mr. Song's words."

"You got valuable information for your investigation, but the truth is that you're only a witness to Chinese justice."

"So you and Mr. Song used me to get information for your case, and now I can't put a period at the end of it. Do you think it's fair that no one outside of Chinatown will ever know what happened to this bum?"

"Maybe."

"Will Mr. Song tell me, at least for old times' sake?"

"No one speaks for Mr. Song. You will have to ask him."

"At least tell me what the deal is with tiger bone wine."

"The wine is made from tiger bones and is an ancient Chinese remedy for an assortment of maladies and bad karma. Drinking it is supposed to give a person strength and special powers to fight adversity. It is also supposed to cure things like arthritis."

"Fair to say that Min Fu-Hok wanted it to give him the power to fight off what you all seem to agree is going to happen to him."

"Seems pretty obvious, doesn't it?"

"Do they kill the tigers to get their bones, or do they use them only after they die of natural causes?"

"As of now, a little of both, but if China ever becomes prosperous again, I'm afraid the tiger is doomed."

"You mean there won't be enough tigers in China to satisfy the demand?"

"With China's large population and the ancient belief in the power of the wine, there won't be enough tigers in the world to satisfy the demand."

"How will the Chinese get tiger bones from other countries?"

"I imagine that in the beginning they will buy them, but when other countries close their borders to those purchases, unscrupulous traffickers will pay poachers to get them by any means possible."

"Doesn't sound too good for the tigers," said Samuel.

20

The Man in Black

SAMUEL AND BERNARDI WERE seated at the Round Table at Camelot, having a drink and discussing the events of the past few weeks.

"Any clue about what happened to Min Fu-Hok?" asked Bernardi.

"Probably nothing good," said Samuel.

"I'll have to have a talk with Mr. Song then," said Bernardi. "The idea of vigilante justice can't be tolerated in a society based on the rule of law."

"I agree with you in principle," said Samuel. "But it won't do you any good to talk to Mr. Song. He won't answer any of your questions. Let me try again with Melody, and we'll talk about this later." Samuel took a drink of his Scotch and set the glass back on the table. "Let's talk about the man in black George told me about."

"I'm ready to haul him in and start asking him some hard questions," said Bernardi.

"Before you do that, can we try a couple of things?" said Samuel. He then proceeded to tell Bernardi his plan, explaining the importance of timing.

"I like your idea," said Bernardi. "I'll get to it the first thing in the morning."

* * *

Bernardi was a man of his word. Around noon the next day, he picked up the phone and called George's number. The pimp wasn't up yet so Bernardi left a message for him to return his call. Around two that afternoon, he did.

"Hello, George. Thanks for calling me back."

"Always nice to hear from you, Lieutenant. What can I do for you?"

"You remember the tip you gave me on Noel Quackenbush?"

"Sure do. How did that turn out? Is he your man in black?"

"Don't know yet. So far I'm out the hundred bucks I gave you, and I don't have much to show for it. But I want you to do me another favor, and there's another twenty in it for you."

"Let's hear what the favor is, Lieutenant, and then we'll talk about money."

"All I want you to do is call Quackenbush on Wednesday and tell him that I'm snooping around, asking about him. And I don't have to tell you, if he asks you, you deny you've given me any information."

George laughed. "I know you wouldn't kill the goose that lays the golden egg. But let's add a little incentive to this obviously important matter. I'll make the phone call for you for twenty bucks, but if I'm successful in getting ahold of him on any Wednesday, let's make it thirty bucks, and if I get ahold of him and pass the message this Wednesday, let's make it fifty bucks."

"You drive a hard bargain, George. I see now I need to start my bargaining at a lower figure when I ask you for information."

"The second step is always more expensive than the first, because the fact that you're back lets me know that the first step is important."

"We won't really know that until we get the results of the phone call."

"Deal or no deal, Lieutenant?"

"It's a deal. I'll deliver the twenty bucks myself within an hour, and then I'll wait for a successful outcome before I pay you the big money."

"Since today is Wednesday, don't go too far from the phone," said George.

"I'll wait at your place to see if you reach him this afternoon."

Bernardi drove to Oakland, made the payment and waited while George called Quackenbush. Bernardi was on the line as well, listening in on the conversation.

"Noel," said George to whoever answered, "I have some news you may be interested in."

"What might that be?" said a suspicious voice.

"Rumor has it that Lieutenant Bernardi of San Francisco Homicide is snooping around, asking a lot of questions about you."

There was a long silence at the other end. "Who'd you hear that from?" Bernardi noticed that man's voice had suddenly climbed an octave higher.

"From my sources, and since we do a little business together, you and I, I thought you'd like to know."

"Yeah, I do appreciate the information," said the man. "I'll be in touch."

George hung up and turned to Bernardi. "There you are, Lieutenant. You got your message delivered, and now I get my fifty bucks." He smiled.

Bernardi shook his hand, reached into his pocket for his wad of bills and peeled off two twenties and a ten.

* * *

Bernardi borrowed George's phone and called Samuel. "Everything went according to plan. I listened in on the conversation."

"That's all I need to know," said Samuel. "Let me double-check that I have the right address."

Bernardi read him Quackenbush's address and phone number.

"Okay," said the reporter. "I'll keep you posted."

Samuel got hold of his photographer, Marcel Fabreceaux, who had moved over to the afternoon paper with Samuel—and who owned the '47 Ford that got Samuel around on his assignments. Samuel confirmed that the plan was a go, and asked Marcel meet him at six. Together with a rookie police officer Bernardi had assigned them, they drove to a modest neighborhood in east Oakland, coming to a halt on MacArthur Boulevard at Highland. Once they had confirmed they were in the right place, they checked the alleyways behind the houses, ascertaining where the residents placed their trash cans for the Thursday morning pickup. Samuel had learned something from Jimmy Shu, the Chinatown bookkeeper, and he wanted to see if it paid off with Noel Quackenbush.

"All we have to do is wait until it gets dark and start checking the trash cans," Samuel explained once Marcel had parked the car at the entrance to the alley behind Quackenbush's house. "We know that Quackenbush is home. Let's just hope he takes out his trash out the night before instead of in the morning. If he does, we can get to work. And if we do find anything, you, Officer, are our witness that it came from his address."

They were in luck. At about nine o'clock they watched as a short, bald-headed man opened the back gate of the address they'd been given. Using a flashlight to guide his way, he placed a single trash can in the alleyway and returned to the house, closing the gate behind him.

Samuel let fifteen minutes pass. "Drive down to where we saw him put the stuff into the trash can." Once they were in position, the glow of a distant streetlight casting its dim light on the scene, Samuel jumped out of the car. "Open the trunk and take out the black plastic bags," he told Marcel. "Officer, you come with me," he said. "I want you to hold one of the bags open." Moving quickly, careful to make as little noise as possible, Samuel picked up the trash can and dumped its contents into the black plastic bag.

"Throw the bag in the trunk and let's get the hell out of here!" he said. Marcel took off down the alley.

"Stop at that Associated gas station on the corner there," shouted an excited Samuel as they wheeled down MacArthur towards the Bay Bridge. "I need to use the payphone." He got out, called Bernardi at home and told him what had happened, and that they were on their way back to his Bryant Street office.

When they arrived they took the black plastic bag up to Homicide. "Dump the contents on the table of the conference room," said Samuel. "We have to catalogue everything that comes out." As Samuel identified each item, the officer who'd accompanied him on the garbage can raid listed and tagged it, signing his name and writing his badge number on all official documents. They then turned the evidence list over to Bernardi.

* * *

A week later, Samuel watched from behind a two-way mirror as Noel Quackenbush waited in the interrogation room at police headquarters. Sitting at the table, his legs stretched nonchalantly under it, he struck Samuel as one cool customer. Looking at his rap sheet, Samuel surmised that Quackenbush was used to playing the question and answer game with police.

After Quackenbush had been waiting about half an hour, Bernardi walked in and sat down on the opposite side of the table, his back to Samuel. He placed his notepad on the table and tossed a file in front of the suspect. The name GRACE CONKLIN was written in bold black letters across the front of the file; Quackenbush could have no doubts as to why he'd been hauled in for questioning. After a moment, the door opened again, and an officer brought in a tape recorder and a pack of Parliament cigarettes. The officer plugged in the tape recorder, dropped the pack on the table.

Bernardi nodded, turned on the tape recorder and introduced himself, explaining that he wanted to ask some questions about the murder of Grace Conklin.

The bald man put his hands on the table and leaned forward. "Don't know who that is, Lieutenant," he said in a soft voice, "so I can't be of much help to you."

"We'll see about that," answered Bernardi. "Can I have your full name, just for the record? I want you to understand that I'm recording this interview for our mutual protection. I don't want either of us to put words in one another's mouth if they weren't actually spoken." He paused. "You say you didn't know Grace Conklin? Have you ever heard the name before?"

"No, sir."

"Don't watch TV or read the papers, or even listen to the radio?"

"Sometimes I listen to the radio."

"Radio? What radio station do you listen to?"

"Mostly rock-n-roll, and sometimes late-night jazz."

"Grace Conklin was murdered a few months ago," said Bernardi, giving him the exact date. "Where were you on that evening?"

"Sitting here with you today, I don't have the slightest idea, Lieutenant. I could ask you the same question and it's only because you prepared this interview that you even know the date."

"Let's change the subject for a moment," said Bernardi. "Where do you bank, Mr. Quackenbush?"

"Security Pacific. Right down the street from my house."

"Do you deposit your paychecks in that bank?"

Quackenbush showed the first signs of concern, Samuel thought, pausing a few seconds before he answered. "No, sir. Those checks I deposit in Crocker National Bank."

"What kind of work do you do, Mr. Quackenbush?"

"I'm a longshoreman, when there is work."

"And when there isn't?"

"I get unemployment. And, just to be honest, sometimes I work as a bartender for cash under the table."

"What do you use the Hibernia Bank for?" asked Bernardi.

"I don't do any banking at Hibernia. I had a car loan there a few years ago, but I paid it off."

"Really?" Bernardi pushed a button and an officer came into the room. The lieutenant whispered something in his ear and the man left the room, returning a moment later with an envelope. Bernardi opened the envelope and took out what looked like a number of bank statements. "You have used the name Myron Schultz in the past, haven't you?"

"Many years ago, when I first came to California."

"According to our records, you've used the name Myron Schultz as an alias, and you even did time under that name ten years ago."

"As I said, that was many years ago."

"But I'm looking at two deposits by Myron Schultz in the Hibernia Bank, one a month before Grace Conklin was murdered and one a week after she was murdered. Both are for five thousand dollars cash."

"Not by me, Lieutenant."

"Come on now, Mr. Quackenbush. Or is it Mr. Schultz? Which do you prefer?"

Bernardi's question was met with a blank stare and silence.

"I took your mug shot down to the bank and two different tellers identified you as a frequent customer there. In fact, you have a history of making ongoing withdrawals from that account, starting two weeks after Grace Conklin's murder."

"It wasn't me, I tell you."

"Let's talk about Parliament cigarettes. Do you smoke 'em?"

"No sir, I've never been a smoker of Parliament or any other brand." Quackenbush smiled, and Samuel, glancing up from his note-taking, thought he detected a look of relief. But the reporter knew the best was yet to come, and he wondered how Quackenbush would try to wriggle out of what was being thrown at him. So far, Samuel felt he hadn't done a very good job of it—no doubt because he never thought they could have compiled so much evidence against him.

"Do you know anybody who smokes them?" asked Bernardi.

"Working as a bartender, I'm sure I've seen a few patrons smoke 'em."

"I don't mean someone who uses them casually. I mean do you know someone you do business with who smokes this particular brand?"

"No, sir. Can't think of a soul."

"How about the man who gave you ten thousand dollars to kill Grace Conklin? We know he smokes Parliaments. Who is he?"

"I don't have the slightest idea what you're talking about, Lieutenant," said Quackenbush. Although he remained outwardly calm, Samuel thought he saw his face flush.

"You want to take the rap for a lousy ten thousand dollars

and maybe go to the gas chamber while Daddy Warbucks rides off into the sunset a free man?"

"You don't have anything on me, Lieutenant." Quackenbush moved to stand. "Am I free to go?"

"Not just yet. I'm not through discussing the evidence with you." Bernardi pushed the button again, and the officer reappeared. The lieutenant didn't bother to whisper this time. "Bring in some more of the stuff," he said.

The officer returned with a wrapped package, a police tag affixed to the side. Bernardi unwrapped the package and pulled out a pair of black pants and a black shirt. "Do these belong to you, Mr. Quackenbush?"

"Never seen them before in my life."

"We pulled them out of your trash can a week ago."

Quackenbush turned pale.

"How about this blond wig? Is that yours?"

"No sir, never seen it before."

"We found it in your trash as well," said Bernardi. "It matches some strands of synthetic material we found at the murder scene." Bernardi leaned back and studied the man across the table. "The noose is tightening, Mr. Quackenbush. Are you ready to give him up, whoever he is?"

"I'm telling you, this is a frame-up. I need to know who set me up. I want a lawyer!"

"One more thing," said Bernardi. "We did a drawing based on your mug shot and placed blond hair and a black hat on the head. And guess what? The Japanese couple at the flower mart identified you as the person who bought daisies the afternoon that Grace Conklin was killed."

"I'm through talking, Lieutenant. I want a lawyer. I have rights, you know."

"Plenty of time to get a lawyer, Mr. Quackenbush. Right now, I'm placing you under arrest for the murder of Grace Conklin." Bernardi pushed the button twice. This time two officers came into the room. "Cuff 'im boys, and book him for murder one."

* * *

After Quackenbush had been carted off, Samuel went into the interrogation room. "Nailed the bastard, huh?"

"Thanks to your hard work, Samuel. Without the evidence you gathered from his trash can and from everywhere else, we would never have solved this crime."

Samuel shrugged. "It's not over yet. We still have to find the bastard who paid him. That is big story here."

"You don't think it was Conklin? He took large sums of money out of his Bank of America account, and we know he had more than enough cash on hand to pay off this jerk both before and after Grace was killed."

Samuel shook his head. "I don't think so. He didn't have a motive to kill her. Jealousy wasn't enough. It's true the marriage was in shambles, and he knew that Jim Abernathy wanted to get rid of him as a son-in-law, but Conklin had it made. He'd already made his dough and his business operation was going full steam ahead. With this Vietnam situation building up, he was set to make a fortune selling Agent Orange, which is used in the defoliation of the jungle."

"So, where do we go from here?" asked Bernardi.

"We need to flush out the man who met Grace Conklin at the motel where she rented a room once a week. I'll start by writing an article about Quackenbush's arrest. I'm relieved you didn't disclose all the clues in your questioning, because the person who hired Quackenbush doesn't know what else we have that may implicate him. I'll make it sound like we have our man, but we can make the paymaster nervous by mentioning the mysterious deposit of ten thousand dollars in Quackenbush's bank account. I'll stay silent about any hard clues we have that may link him to the murder."

After they finished their conversation, Samuel went back to his office to write his article for the afternoon paper. Before he started, however, he called Jim Abernathy to tell him that Quackenbush had been arrested.

"Is that the end of it?" asked Abernathy, disappointed that Conklin hadn't been implicated.

"I don't think so. We still need to find out who paid Quackenbush to commit murder."

"So Conklin is not out of the picture?"

"He's not out of the picture," said Samuel, "but no matter what you thought of him, he didn't have a motive. That's all I can say for the moment, but as soon as I get a break in the case, you'll be one of the first to know."

He hung up the phone and wrote his headline:

Alleged Murderer of Grace Abernathy Captured

The article gave details of the evidence that had been collected against Quackenbush and how the clues had implicated him. It disclosed nothing, however, about what the authorities knew about the paymaster, other than to note that the alleged murderer had deposited an unexplained payment of ten thousand dollars in one of his bank accounts.

21

Who Got the Dough?

SAMUEL, BERNARDI AND CHARLES Perkins sat in a conference room down the hall from Bernardi's office, looking over piles of bank records. They were copies of the statements that had been used at Min Fu-Hok's hearing at Mr. Song's Many Chinese Herbs shop. Also included was Mrs. Wuan's affidavit, along with the deposit slip for the gold that had been sent to a numbered Swiss bank account.

Charles Perkins was only there because he was eager to see if Min Fu-Hok's criminal activities had taken place on an international scale. He hoped to prove there had been a conspiracy involving the illegal movement of big money and gold, which would bring him not only a conviction, but also major headlines.

Samuel held up the deposit slips to the numbered Swiss account. "Min Fu-Hok deposited at least a hundred thousand dollars in Switzerland, as well as an equivalent amount of gold bullion. And that's not all. Another hundred thousand went into a Swiss account from Conklin's Bank of America account."

Perkins beamed, proud to have been responsible for the subpoena that uncovered that transaction. "I betcha those two were in on a big illegal scheme," he said.

"The argument we first used was that Min Fu-Hok was sheltering money to protect it in case he was sued by all the families in Chinatown whose relatives he killed," said Bernardi.

"That answers the question for him, but it doesn't explain why Conklin would also deposit money in Switzerland," said Samuel. "Is there any way to tell if it went into the same account?"

"Impossible to tell right now, and we may never know, because of Switzerland's secrecy laws," said Perkins. "We need to explore another angle. It's my hunch that the two were involved in something together."

"What does Min Fu-Hok have to say about all this?" asked Bernardi.

"He wouldn't talk," said Samuel. "He was given a chance, but he said nothing."

"Tell me where he is, and I'll haul him in for questioning," said Perkins.

"Can't be done," said Samuel.

"Why not?"

"Because no one can find him."

"You said there was some kind of a trial," said Perkins. "What was the outcome?"

"He was found guilty by Mr. Song," said Samuel.

"And what was the sentence?"

"We couldn't find out."

"What do you mean you couldn't find out?"

"Every day I go back and inquire and I get the same answer—that it's still under advisement."

"We'll haul Mr. Song in and ask him," said Perkins.

"Ask him what?" said Samuel. "He's done nothing wrong."

"Ask him where Min Fu-Hok is."

"Do you think he would tell you anything, after what you

did to his shop a couple of years ago?" said Samuel angrily, standing up and pointing a menacing finger at him.

"What do you mean?" asked Perkins, feigning innocence. "I was just doing my job."

"Never mind. Take my word for it. You'd be wasting your time."

"What about Min Fu-Hok's wife?" suggested Perkins. "Let's go to her shop and take her into custody."

"Her shop is shuttered and she's disappeared as well," said Samuel. "Apparently, she's left the country."

"Didn't she have to forfeit her passport?" asked Perkins.

"That was her husband," answered Samuel. "She wasn't charged with or convicted of anything."

"Is there any way we can get to the bottom of this?" asked Bernardi.

"That's a question for Charles," said Samuel. "There is so much secrecy surrounding Swiss numbered accounts that we, as ordinary investigators, can't get that information. The only agency left with power to inquire is the federal government."

Perkins stood up, rubbing his clammy hands together, then wiped them on his shiny blue pants, which had long ago lost their creases. "I wish it were that easy," he said with an uncharacteristic show of humility. "Uncle Sam doesn't have the power you think he does when it comes to getting to the bottom of where international money is hidden."

Samuel smiled, amused by Perkins's change in attitude. "The way I see it, there are at least two possibilities. One is that Conklin was putting money in Min Fu-Hok's account because he was facing what could have been a serious financial hit if he were to be charged in the death of one of his employees, and he was paying the freight for Min Fu-Hok to hide it for him."

"That makes a lot of sense," agreed Bernardi.

"There's another possibility, though," said Samuel. "And

that is that both men were putting money into a secret account for some other reason, and we just don't know what it is right now. We'll just have to look further to see if there is, in fact, some connection between them."

"That one's on you, Samuel," said Perkins, regaining his haughty demeanor. "It's a long shot, and I bet you don't even know where to start." He stretched his arms restlessly and stood up. "I've done enough for you fellows. Now I have to get back to work. I'll find out if the money and the gold went to the same bank, but that's as much as I can do." He put his copies of the subpoenaed records from the Bank of America in his briefcase and walked out of the room without even saying goodbye.

"Where does that leave us?" asked Bernardi as the door closed behind Perkins. "We don't know where to go from here on this issue."

"It's not where you start," said Samuel, "it's where you end up. I think there is a connection between those three deposits and the two that went to Quackenbush. Our job is to find it."

"Do you also feel that the money that went into Quackenbush's account is relevant to the other deposits and to the gold?" asked Bernardi.

"There's a big difference between a few thousand bucks and the amount that was moved from local banks to the Swiss numbered accounts," said Samuel. "Like I said, our job is to make the connection."

22

The Halls Come Tumbling Down

SAMUEL WOKE UP DEPRESSED. He looked out the dirty windows of his small flat on the edge of Chinatown, and even though it was a sunny Saturday morning, he didn't want to get out of bed. He lay there thinking that for him to catch Quackenbush, he needed enough evidence to connect him to the master puppeteer behind Grace's murder. Thinking that person might never be caught upset Samuel, and he knew he had to expose him. All he needed was a break.

Samuel thought about two of the clues not disclosed in his article: the Parliament cigarette butt and the oak leaf, which were both found at the scene of the crime. As he thought back on his investigation, Samuel remembered the motel manager's statement that the man who met Grace Conklin every week smoked Parliaments. That's why Bernardi had left a package of them on the table during his interrogation, hoping that Quackenbush would see them and panic, and later try to get in touch with whoever had hired him. But that hadn't worked; Quackenbush was too seasoned a criminal to fall for it. It also didn't help that a lot of people smoked Parliaments, which was a popular brand.

As for the leaf, it would have had no relevance were it not for a similar, inch-square section of leaf found in the cuff of the black pants discovered in Quackenbush's trash. Scientific analysis showed the two samples came from the same tree. But there were thousands of oak trees in the Bay Area. The odds of Samuel finding the one that the two leaves came from was almost zero. Where would he start?

He dialed Bernardi's home number, "Hi, Bruno this is Samuel."

"What's up, Samuel?" asked Bernardi, setting down his coffee.

"I need to talk to you about Grace's case. Can you meet me at Camelot around noon?"

"How long do you think it will take? I promised Marisol I'd take her sailing this afternoon."

"I didn't know you were a sailor, Bruno."

"I'm not, and it's a long story."

"Good, you can tell it to me."

"Okay," said Bernardi, agreeing to meet him at Camelot around noon.

* * *

As Samuel and Bernardi sat at the Round Table having a cup of coffee, Melba came in the back way, Excalibur in tow, and a lit Lucky Strike. Excalibur shook his tailless fanny when he saw Samuel, and the reporter, fulfilling his role in their ritual, pulled out a dog treat before Excalibur even reached the table.

"Good morning boys," said Melba, who was dressed in white slacks and a chartreuse blouse. She crushed out her cigarette in an ashtray set in the middle of the Round Table. "This must be a big pow-wow. Two of San Francisco's most important sleuths don't get up early on a Saturday morning just for the hell of it."

"We're stuck," said Samuel, quickly filling her in on the

clues that had thus far led nowhere.

"Sounds like a tough one to me," said Melba. "Why don't you take the day off and go to the re-inauguration of the police chief at City Hall. It starts at two. Get your mind off of this crap for a while and take advantage of some free Italian salami and champagne."

"Christ, I forgot about that," said Bernardi. "I have to put in an appearance, for sure. Can I borrow your phone, Melba? I'll have to cancel my sailing date with Marisol."

"Sure, use the one behind the bar."

As Bernardi headed to the horseshoe bar, Samuel called after him, "I'll come along for the ride."

Bernardi nodded absentmindedly; he was more interested in what he was going to say to placate Marisol than in accommodating Samuel.

"By the way," said Melba, watching Bernardi hustle to the phone, "whatever happened with that trial in Chinatown? You never wrote a word about it."

"I can't write the article because the man was condemned, and then he disappeared," said Samuel.

"What do you mean 'disappeared'?"

"Vanished. No one will say what happened to him."

They tossed the problem around for a couple of minutes until Bernardi returned, greatly relieved. "Everything is under control. I'll take her to dinner tonight instead."

When he was again seated, Melba continued her line of questioning. "What about that herbalist? Wasn't he the judge? He should know where the defendant is if he's the one who sentenced him."

"That's what I've been saying," said Bernardi, "but Samuel says he won't talk, and I can't make him."

"I see. I think Samuel is right. Chinese justice has been served. You'll never find out what happened to him."

"Do you think that's right?" said Bernardi.

"It's not a matter of being right or wrong," said Melba. "That's just the way it is in Chinatown."

Samuel sighed. "How can I write an article about a man who was condemned by Mr. Song's tribunal and conclude by saying that no one knows what happened to him?"

"End of story, boys. Go have fun this afternoon."

Melba pulled Excalibur away from the table and headed for her office at the rear of the bar. Samuel and Bernardi called out their goodbyes and left the bar, jumping into Bernardi's Ford Victoria, which was parked just outside.

* * *

On their way to City Hall, Samuel motioned to Bernardi. "Pull over at this phone booth. I need to call Marcel. I want him to meet me at this shindig." He made his phone call and Marcel agreed to get there as soon as he could.

When they arrived, there was already a large crowd of people milling about in front of City Hall, waiting for the doors to open. "Can we wait a few minutes for Marcel to arrive?" Samuel asked. "I'd like him to get some photographs for an article I want to write for the paper."

"Sure," said Bernardi. "I'm not in any hurry." When Marcel arrived a half hour later, they went in together, using Bernardi's shield to gain immediate access.

Once inside, Samuel was intrigued to note the large number of local bureaucrats in attendance. In addition to the entire judiciary, he saw the City Attorney, who was surrounded by a group of men that Samuel assumed were part of his legal staff. He even saw Charles Perkins drinking champagne while he chatted with the District Attorney and a few of his deputies. Among them were Giuseppe Maximiliano, the deputy who had tried Min Fu-Hok, and who also handled Conklin's preliminary hearing. Samuel approached Giuseppe, asking if he knew the whereabouts of Min Fu-Hok.

"Not a clue," Giuseppe responded. "The judge issued a bench warrant for his arrest when he didn't show up to report to his probation officer. Talk to the judge about it, he's right over there." He pointed out Hiram Petersen, who was leaning against the staircase's stone banister chatting and smoking a cigarette.

"I'll get around to asking him, although I doubt if he knows any more about it than you do," said Samuel, not wanting to say anything about what had transpired at Mr. Song's. "The man just seems to have disappeared."

"You know as much as I do," said Giuseppe.

Samuel knew that wasn't true.

When more than two hundred people had gathered in the first floor foyer, the crowd spilling up the marble staircase to the second floor, the chairman of the Board of Supervisors introduced the mayor. He gave a short speech about the painstaking search that had been made to find the right man to serve as police chief, his decision to stick with Thomas Cahill and his eagerness to re-introduce him to the public.

The chief took the microphone next, giving a rousing speech about how he would continue to fight crime and protect the public. It was the same speech Samuel and everyone else had heard time and time again, but Samuel took notes anyway, since he was obligated to write a story on the re-inauguration, even if he didn't much feel like it.

After the speech, there was a celebratory feeling in the air as champagne and hors d'oeuvres were consumed. People gathered in small groups, chatting and congratulating each other for the significant parts they had played (or at least believed they had played) in helping maintain the same chief. They gathered around him, echoing the chorus of well-wishing, wanting most of all to be remembered when they needed something.

Bernardi introduced Samuel to Chief Cahill, describing him as one of the city's top reporters, and adding that Samuel had been very helpful to him and the police department in fighting crime and capturing criminals.

"I know of your work, Mr. Hamilton, and we are grateful here in San Francisco to have you on our team," the chief responded, handing Samuel his business card.

Samuel had Marcel snap a couple of pictures of Bernardi and the chief. Then he and Bernardi moved on to another part of the room, where the judiciary was gathered. After exchanging pleasantries with several judges, Samuel excused himself, dragged Marcel into a corner and whispered something to him. After that, he moved on to chat with members of the Board of Supervisors, as well as the City Attorney.

Within twenty minutes, Marcel came over to Samuel and nodded. Immediately Samuel turned to Bernardi. "We've got to get out of here," he said. "I have important information to share with you."

Bernardi said his perfunctory goodbyes and the three of them left the building, exiting onto Larkin Street.

"Okay," said Samuel to Marcel. "How long will it take you to develop the photos I asked you to take?"

"I'll go downtown and get started right away. Should have them in a couple of hours."

"What's the scoop?" asked Bernardi.

"Just a second," said Samuel. Turning back to Marcel, he asked, "Did you get the other thing I asked for?"

"Sure did." Marcel took something wrapped in a cocktail napkin out of the pocket where he usually kept spent flashbulbs and handed it to Samuel.

Samuel carefully unfolded the napkin and showed Bernardi what was inside. Then he wrapped it back up and gave it to him. "Now you have some more evidence. Will you take me to Homicide, so we can look at the Grace Conklin evidence file?"

"Does this mean what I think it means?" asked Bernardi.

"We won't know until we can compare," said Samuel.

"Let's go now, then," said Bernardi. "Marcel, when you have the photos, come to my office."

* * *

Samuel and Bernardi looked over the evidence from Grace Conklin's murder, which was spread out on the table of the Homicide conference room. They were interested in only one item, however—the Parliament cigarette butt found at the scene of the crime. Bernardi picked it up with tweezers and turned it over a few times. He then looked at the cigarette butt that Samuel had wrapped in the cocktail napkin and handled it the same way, turning it over slowly with the tweezers and considering it from all sides.

"Looking at the photo of the butt taken at the scene and comparing it to the actual butt from the murder scene, and then looking at the one you took from the police chief's inauguration, you can see that they were stubbed out in the same way. See the angle of the crush? Amazing, isn't it? We need to see if the prints we got off the butt at the scene are the same as the ones we take off this one."

A few moments later, Marcel arrived with a small stack of photographs, which he spread out on an empty section of the table.

"You can see him putting out his cigarette in the photo Marcel took. Look closely—it has the same shape as the butt found at the scene of the crime."

"I'll be goddamned," said Bernardi. "If this is our suspect, it's a sad day for the city."

Samuel was growing impatient. "Now we have to see if we can match the oak leaf that was found at the crime scene and the one we found in Quackenbush's pant cuff with an oak tree on our suspect's property. If we can do that, it'll be time to talk to Perkins again."

"Why him?" asked Bernardi.

"Let's see if we can find matching leaves, then we'll talk about Perkins."

"Let's get a search warrant first," said Bernardi.

"I don't think that a search warrant will fly unless we get a fingerprint comparison from the butts or a matching leaf," said Samuel. "Besides, have you thought about what you have to disclose to get a warrant?"

"We can't get an oak leaf that counts without a warrant."

"Just watch me. If you give me the address, Marcel and I can get one," said Samuel. "If the one we get is from the same tree, we can argue that one thing led us to the other."

"How are you going to do that, Samuel?" asked Bernardi.

"Just get me what I need and let me go at it," said Samuel, writing down a list of everything he wanted Bernardi to collect for him. After he had explained his plan, Bernardi smiled. "Definitely worth a try," he said. "You have all day tomorrow."

"I don't think going to a house to pick up oak leaves on a Sunday is a good idea," said Samuel. "We either need some ruse to get everybody out of the house so we don't get shot or arrested as trespassers, or we need to come up with a plausible reason to be there. In the meantime, you have to line up a botanist who can compare what we find with what we already have."

* * *

On Monday morning, Samuel had Marcel drive him to the fashionable address in Hillsborough, which Bernardi had obtained for him. He was dressed in white coveralls with a Hillsborough Fire Department logo on the lapel, and wore a matching cap that Bernardi gotten the local fire department to loan him. It was common knowledge that a fire inspector could enter any house or business without a warrant. He had Marcel park down the street and out of sight, so he wouldn't have to explain to the occupants what a fire inspector was doing driving up in a '47 green Ford coupe.

It was just after ten when he rang the doorbell. An attractive middle-aged woman answered the door. "Good morning, ma'am," he said with a smile. "I'm from the Fire Department. As you may know, this is the time of year we do neighborhood inspections, and I need to check your premises to make sure there are no fire hazards."

"We're not aware of any fire dangers here," she said, "but you're more than welcome to have a look. Right this way. I'll be in the laundry room if you need me. Just knock on the door."

Samuel strolled confidently through the elegantly decorated home, looking for obvious places to hide a safe. He noted three paintings on the walls of the second floor where one might be, and when he was in the study, actually went so far as to look behind two paintings. He spotted what looked like a safe behind one of them.

He went out into the backyard and pretended to examine what he thought was a gardener's shack or tool shed, which he saw had a frayed electric or telephone line leading to it. At the same time, he noted two oak trees and wandered back toward them, trying to give the impression to anyone who might be watching that he was sizing up the problem. He stooped down and picked up leaves from beneath each tree and dropped them in different pockets of his coveralls. When he had what he needed, he knocked at the laundry room door.

"There's no problem with anything on your property, ma'am," he said when she answered. "I'll just let myself out the side gate and be on my way down the street. Thank you for your cooperation."

"You're welcome, young man," she smiled. "It's nice to know we're in compliance."

Samuel went out the side gate, scooping more leaves from the ground beneath the oak tree in the front yard, and went down the street to Marcel's car. "Got what we came for," said Samuel as he slid into the front seat and took off his Hillsborough Fire Department cap. "Back to the city and to the botanist to see if we have a match."

* * *

The next day, Samuel and Bernardi were back in Bernardi's conference room, the evidence still spread out where they had left it a couple of days before. Bernardi had the botanist's report and was reading it aloud to Samuel: " 'Scientific evidence proves that the sample picked up in the front yard is a biological match for the leaf found in the cuff of the pant leg, as well as the leaf found at the crime scene. In short, they all three came from the same tree.' "

Bernardi handed the report to Samuel, so he could see the analysis himself. "Extraordinary work, Samuel," said Bernardi. "Now we have to get a search warrant and look for evidence of other clues in the house itself. We also need to gather more leaves. That should be easy because they're in the front yard."

"Let's go and see Perkins," said Samuel, proceeding to explain why.

"I get it," said Bernardi. "He's such a pain in the ass, though. Can you make the arrangements?"

"I promise, he'll welcome us with open arms," said Samuel. He called Perkins and set up an appointment for that afternoon.

* * *

Charles Perkins greeted them impatiently, as if he knew

something big was about to happen, something that could benefit him. As he ushered Samuel and Bernardi into his conference room—there was nowhere to sit down and have a conversation while examining evidence in his own office—he couldn't resist a triumphant smile. Nonetheless, he tried to play it cool.

"What are you two so excited about?" he asked ingenuously.

"We think we're getting close to blowing this case wide open," said Samuel. "But we need your help."

"We're always here to help," Perkins said. "Sit down and tell me what you want me to do."

Bernardi, who stood behind Perkins, rolled his eyes. Samuel tried to suppress a laugh, but the grin on his face gave him away.

"What's so funny?" asked Perkins.

"Nothing, just one of Bernardi's private jokes," said Samuel.

Perkins ignored the infinite possibilities inherent in that statement, focusing instead on the red meat he sensed was his for the devouring. "Tell me what you want?"

"We're going to show you the evidence we've gathered," said Bernardi, "and then we're going to tell you why we're here." He laid out the Parliament cigarette butt from the murder site, the Parliament cigarette butt from City Hall and the photo of the person in the process of putting the second butt out. "These cigarette butts were both crushed in the same way, and we believe they were crushed by the person pictured in the photo."

"Really?" said Perkins. "That's a pretty serious charge. How can you prove that?"

Bernardi placed the oak leaves found at the murder scene and in the cuff of Quackenbush's pant cuff on the table, followed by the two oak leaves that Samuel had gathered from the front yard in Hillsborough. "A botanist tells us all these oak leaves came from the same tree, which is located in the front yard of this man's house." He showed Perkins the photo of the man putting out the cigarette at the police chief's reappointment ceremony at City Hall, along with a map pinpointing the location of the suspect's home in Hillsborough.

"For obvious reasons, we need the federal government to issue the search warrant," said Samuel.

"What are we waiting for?" asked Perkins.

"You," said Samuel and Bernardi, looking at each other knowingly. They knew what was coming. It hadn't yet registered with Perkins.

* * *

The next day, U.S. Marshals bearing search warrants descended on Judge Hiram Peterson's chambers at the Hall of Justice and at his home in Hillsborough, looking for any evidence of Swiss bank accounts. Perkins led the team that went to his chambers, Bernardi at his side. Three U.S. Marshals were on hand to serve the warrant.

Perkins was red faced and trembling with rage, and why not? He had worked with the judge as a prosecutor in the U. S. Attorney's office; Peterson was as much a friend as Perkins was capable of making. But from the evidence Perkins had seen, Peterson had crossed the line, shamed the profession and violated his solemn oath of office. Perkins wanted to look Peterson in the eye while he searched for evidence to use against him, and he wanted the judge to know that he had an enemy dedicated to putting him away for a long time.

Bernardi saw what was developing and grabbed Perkins by the arm as the marshal told the court clerk to announce them to the judge. "We need you to keep cool right now, Charles. You need to explain to him what we want and see if he gives it up voluntarily."

"That son of a bitch," Perkins said under his breath. Although he managed to internalize his rage, his face remained bright red. He was clearly shaken, and if Bernardi hadn't intervened, a shouting match would surely have followed, and very likely nothing would have been accomplished.

The clerk notified the judge that federal officers wanted to see him. A minute later, word came back that they were all invited into the judge's chambers. Judge Peterson was sitting at his desk, smoking a cigarette and drinking a cup of coffee. He rose to greet them, his demeanor giving nothing away. In fact, he looked like a fashion model posing as a jurist, one who had stepped right out of the pages of *Esquire* magazine.

"Gentlemen, what can I do for you?"

Perkins paused a moment, trying to control himself. "On behalf of the United States Government, we're here to serve this search warrant on you," he said. "After you've had a chance to read it, we will give you an opportunity to give up the evidence we are requesting. If you surrender it, we will then have to check to see if you've withheld anything. If you deny the existence of the evidence that we suspect is in your possession or under your control, we will use this warrant to search for it." Perkins mentioned nothing about the marshals currently searching his home; Peterson would find that out soon enough.

After he read the affidavit attached to the search warrant Peterson said, "I think it's appropriate for me to call my lawyer. I'd also like to call my wife."

"You can call your lawyer," said Charles, still angry that the jurist had sullied the reputation of the judiciary, "and you can call your wife, but we will listen in on your conversations. And we will not halt the search until he gets here, which we assume you are going to ask us to do. And if you try to tell your wife to destroy or hide any evidence in your home, we will immediately arrest you for interfering with our investigation."

"Since you won't stop this nonsense, why should I bother having my lawyer come down here at all?" Peterson said, standing up and prissily smoothing one of the sleeves of his expensive gray suit. "However, please don't try and question me in his absence." He seemed to be talking more to himself than anyone else.

The marshals removed the contents of the judge's desk, the pictures on his walls and the law books from his bookcases. They also tore up the carpet to see what might be underneath. Then they went into his courtroom and removed the contents of both his desk and his clerk's desk, opening every drawer and turning it over to see if there were any notes stuck to bottom.

"We're leaving now," said Perkins when he and Bernardi were ready to go. "We advise you to stay away from your home until our team is finished there. I also advise you not to interfere with that search either."

The judge looked like a trapped animal. His eyes searched the room furtively, as if looking for an escape, though there was none to be had. He had obviously been surprised by the arrival of Perkins and the marshals. If the search warrants had been obtained through the San Francisco police department, rather than Perkins and the federal court, there would have been a leak, and he would have found out about it in enough time to make any evidence disappear.

* * *

Samuel was with the team of marshals that descended on Peterson's Hillsborough home. When the U.S. Marshal presented her with the search warrant, Peterson's wife caught sight of Samuel and exclaimed, "My goodness, you're the fireman! What's going on? I need to call my husband. He's a superior court judge in San Francisco."

"That won't be necessary, ma'am," explained the marshal. "I'm afraid you will have to stand aside while we do our work."

Looking confused, Mrs. Peterson retreated to the den, one marshal at her side and another listening in on an extension line as she dialed the judge. She frowned as she put the phone down. "My husband said to cooperate with you," she said, looking more nonplused than ever and collapsing into the chair by the phone.

Samuel led the marshals into the room where he'd seen the safe. One of the marshals gathered the papers from the top of the desk and then from the drawers. "Will you give us the combination to this safe, ma'am?" he asked.

"I'm afraid I don't know it," she said.

"That's too bad, because if I can't open it, I'll have to rip it out of the wall, and you know what a mess that will make."

"Let me call my husband and ask him."

After a short discussion over the phone, she picked up a pen, wrote some numbers on a notepad and hung up the phone. The marshal took the notepad and, using rubber gloves, opened the safe. He then removed the contents, taking notes as he went.

"Anything interesting?" Samuel asked.

"Won't know until we get this stuff downtown."

Samuel walked over to another marshal in the process of collecting papers from the desk. Taking the man aside, he said, "Better look on the bottom of the drawers. There may be something pasted there."

The marshal removed each drawer from the desk and turned it over. Sure enough, pasted to the bottom of the last drawer on the right was a small sheet of paper. He carefully removed it and put it in an envelope, making note of exactly where he'd found it.

The remaining marshals scoured the house, looking for documents and other evidence, and consulting with Samuel as necessary.

"Don't forget to scoop up handfuls of leaves from the front and back yards," said Samuel. "When you're done, meet me at the garden shed at the rear of the property. There are some piles of dirt we need to go through carefully. We also need to check and see if there are any signs of holes dug anywhere in the yard where something could be hidden. Did any of you bring a metal detector?"

No one had.

"Contact the Hillsborough police or even the San Mateo Sherriff's office and ask them if they have one you can borrow," said Samuel. "I won't feel finished with this place until I know you've gone over every inch of it."

The youngest marshal nodded in agreement. "While you and my colleague are looking through the garden shed, I'll go down the hill and see what I can find."

Samuel and the marshal looked through the shed for over an hour but found nothing of interest. While they were searching, the young officer returned with a metal detector, a contraption with a circular disk at the end of a pole and wires leading to a meter near the handle. The team moved the metal detector across the floor of the shed, careful to keep the disk a couple inches off the ground, but there was no response so they moved to the backyard garden. As they passed over the ground near a row of rosebushes, there was a slight jump in the meter's needle. One of the marshals ran to get a shovel and garden trowel from the shed.

"Be careful how you dig there," advised Samuel.

Instead of using the shovel, the man got down on his hands and knees and gently inserted the trowel into the soft dirt. He hit something almost immediately, and quickly removed the dirt from around it. It was a canning jar with a metal top, the kind Samuel had seen his grandmother use to cook and store vegetables and fruits for the long Nebraska winter months. The marshal pulled it out of the ground and wiped it off, and they peered through the glass to see what was inside. The jar appeared to be filled wads of one hundred dollar bills.

"The top is rusty," said Samuel. "We'll have to have an expert remove it so we don't break it." The head marshal put the jar in a box he had set aside for any items taken from the garden.

They continued their search with the metal detector, and on the other side of the garden, under an oak tree, they got another hit, this time deeper underground. The marshall took the shovel and began digging. After removing nearly a foot of dirt, they saw the top of another canning jar. The marshal used the trowel to expose a quart jar, this one filled with documents in French.

"Do you read French?" the marshal asked Samuel.

"Not enough to figure out what it says," said Samuel. "But if I had to guess, I'd say they look like bank receipts."

* * *

Three days later, Samuel, Bernardi, the San Francisco District Attorney, his top deputy and several federal officials—including the U.S. Attorney, two forensic scientists and an attorney from the U.S. State Department, an expert in international banking—sat in Charles' conference room, surrounded by boxes of evidence that had been taken from the judge's chambers and home.

"Does any of what was picked up confirm Peterson had a secret bank account in Switzerland?" asked Samuel.

"Yes, sir," said State Department attorney. "He has one, all right. Now the question is, how much does he have in it and where did it come from?"

Samuel spoke first. "We know that Min Fu-Hok deposited a hundred thousand somewhere. And it looks like almost that entire amount went into Peterson's account."

"How do you know Min Fu-Hok sent a hundred grand to a Swiss bank account?" asked Perkins.

"From the copies of the bank records Jimmy Shu provided, and from Mrs. Wuan's affidavit, both of which I gave you," said Samuel.

"I hadn't forgotten that," said Perkins, feigning calm, though Samuel could see his fists were clenched. "Just trying to fit it all together. In addition to that, I have records from the Bank of America, which show a similar deposit from Conklin into a Swiss bank account in the amount of another hundred thousand dollars. So the question to you, Mr. Expert, is how do we show that this money ended up in Peterson's secret bank account?"

"From the papers found in the glass jar, it looks like a hundred thousand went into that account," said the State Department attorney. "We were able to determine that he then withdrew twenty thousand."

"So he used ten thousand to pay off Quackenbush," said Perkins, "and the other ten thousand was hidden in the jar."

"Wait a minute," said the U.S. Attorney. "How do you know that?"

"Peterson withdrew twenty thousand from the account," answered Perkins. "But there was only ten thousand in the jar. We deduced that he used the other ten thousand to pay off Quackenbush."

"What else do you have on this Quackenbush character?" asked the U.S. Attorney.

"Enough to get him to rat on the judge for a lighter sentence," said the District Attorney.

"What do you have on the judge besides the bribe?" asked the U.S. Attorney.

"We'll charge him as an accessory to murder," said the District Attorney. "His cigarette butt at the scene of the crime and the oak leaf found in Quackenbush's pant cuff are a start."

"Is that enough to turn Quackenbush?" asked Samuel.

"The combination might be," said Bernardi. "You never know what will break a con like Quackenbush. But the argument is, why take the whole rap when he can make a deal and serve less time? He knows how the system works."

The U.S. Attorney stood up. "I think you have enough to charge him with bribery at the state level. We can also charge him for trying to hide it for illegal purposes at the federal level, and of course for failure to pay tax on it. The District Attorney and Charles here should have a talk with his lawyer and tell him what's coming. If Quackenbush is convicted of bribery and accessory to murder, he won't see the outside of jail for the rest of his life. And if federal crimes are added on, he'll serve two lifetime sentences."

"Don't you think that Peterson knows that without his cooperation, we'll never get the complete details about the Swiss bank account, and without access to the account, we can't show he actually got the money?" said Perkins.

"With the papers you found in his backyard, we can make a pretty good circumstantial case that he's got the money," said the U.S. Attorney.

Samuel stood up, shaking his head vehemently. "It's more than circumstantial," he argued. "His name and fingerprints are on the documents. Plus, there's a withdrawal slip for twenty thousand, as well as the ten thousand in cash we found in the jar."

He sat back down and turned to Perkins. "But I have an even bigger question. Can I write an article about this now?"

"We'll charge Peterson tomorrow with the state crimes and then you can," said the District Attorney.

Perkins bowed his head, his face red. He hated not being

in charge of the process.

"What about the federal charges, though?" asked Samuel, trying to throw Perkins a bone.

Perkins, quickly recovering his bravado, smiled. But before he was able to answer, the District Attorney intervened again. "Just say they're pending."

Samuel, feeling sorry for Perkins, tried again. "What do you think, Charles?"

"That'll do it," said Perkins, clearly unhappy to have had his power usurped.

"Are you sure?" asked Samuel, thinking back to the argument they'd had on the sidewalk outside Perkins's office when he and Barry Fong-Torres had first approached him about the case.

"Yeah, that'll work," said Perkins pompously, doing his best to reestablish some sense of authority. "I'll give you more details later so you can quote me."

* * *

There was one last piece of business to attend to. Samuel and Bernardi drove down to the waterfront to see Jim Abernathy. After a cursory glance, the black-clad security guard recognized them and opened the gate. They climbed the stairs to the building, which faced the Oakland Estuary, and entered Abernathy's office, saying hello to Agnes, the brown-haired secretary and informing her that they had an appointment with the boss. She nodded and announced their arrival.

Abernathy came out into the reception area to greet them. "Glad to see you fellows. Do you have news for me?"

"Yes sir, we do," said Bernardi.

"Come on inside and sit down," said Abernathy, ushering them into his office, his expression anticipatory.

"Can I offer ye a drink?" he asked once they were seated

around his large rosewood desk.

"Too early in the day for me," said Bernardi.

"I'll have to take a rain check," said Samuel. "I'm on deadline for an article that goes to press this afternoon, which is actually why we're here."

"Does this article have to do with what I think it does?" He looked at them apprehensively.

"Yes, sir, it does," said Bernardi. "We've arrested your daughter's killer."

Abernathy turned pale. "So it wasn't Conklin after all, 'cause he's dead."

"No, it wasn't him," said Bernardi. "I'm sorry to tell you this, but your daughter's lover had her killed."

"You're kidding me, of course," said Abernathy, wide-eyed with disbelief.

"I'm afraid not," said Samuel. "Judge Hiram Peterson hired a thug to do the job for ten thousand dollars. And in case you didn't know, Conklin paid the judge a hundred grand to find in his favor in the criminal charges that were brought against Conklin in the death of his employee. It was at the same time the judge was having an affair with your daughter, and from what I have been able to put together, he must have felt that his relationship with her was too close for comfort once he got the big money offer from Conklin. So he decided to get rid of her. Or maybe she learned that he was the judge in her husband's case, and tried to put pressure on him. The truth is, we'll never know for sure unless Peterson tells us, and it's doubtful he will."

"A judge did this?" said Abernathy, stunned. His eyes filled with tears.

"I'm afraid so, Mr. Abernathy. We wanted you to know all this before Mr. Hamilton published his article this afternoon about the judge's arrest."

Abernathy wiped his eyes with his handkerchief and

poured himself a tumbler of Irish whiskey. He lifted the bottle in their direction, once again offering them a drink. Samuel and Bernardi acquiesced; it seemed churlish not to join the man in a toast. Abernathy poured each of them a tumbler and all three solemnly clinked glasses.

"To my daughter, God rest her soul," said Abernathy.

*　*　*

The afternoon paper's front page beamed the news in big block letters:

PROMINENT LOCAL JUDGE CHARGED WITH BRIBERY AND ACCESSORY TO MURDER. FEDERAL CHARGES EXPECTED

As soon as the scandal hit the streets, Samuel's phone began ringing off the hook. The AP had gotten hold of the story, and since judicial corruption was always a hot item nationwide, other news outlets were hungry for details. Samuel spent the rest of the day working on several in-depth articles to be shared with his fellow reporters. He finished up around seven, when he decided it was time head over to Camelot.

Excalibur was waiting for him at his usual spot at the Round Table, and as Samuel gave the dog his treat, Melba shot him a triumphant smile and Blanche beamed from behind the horseshoe bar. They'd obviously already read the newspaper.

"Another victory, Samuel," said Melba, laughing. "Now you can get your old job back at the morning paper."

"They've already offered to double my salary and give me a column if I want it," said Samuel, a self-satisfied look on his face.

"And of course you said no—playing hard to get, right?" she teased, lighting another Lucky Strike.

"I told them I'd think about it. They treated me badly, and

if I went back to work for them, I'd always have that in the back of my mind."

"Think of twice the money you're making now and then think of that shithole you live in," said Melba. "That should make up your mind."

"Yeah, I know. But I'm not in a hurry. They could have offered me my job back a long time ago. But they waited until Conklin was out of the way. I don't like that."

"Enough of that for now," said Melba, exhaling smoke through her nose. "Have a drink and let's celebrate."

Blanche brought Samuel a Scotch on the rocks and gave him a kiss on the cheek. He lifted his drink in a toast and Melba and Blanche joined him, raising glasses of beer and carrot juice, respectively.

"Why do you think a judge with a bright future like his would take bribes and become an accessory to murder?" asked Blanche.

"I've asked myself that question many times since we cornered him," said Samuel.

"In ten years a shrink will tell the parole board that his mother didn't love him, so please let him out of jail," said Melba. "But the truth is that asshole has no character."

"I agree with you. But how did he fool so many people for so long?"

"He hijacked the good name that his education and political connections gave him, is all," said Melba. "There are a lot of pricks around the city like him. Most never get caught. He just overstepped his bounds."

Everyone nodded and sipped their drinks in silence for a moment. Perhaps sensing the solemn turn the conversation had taken, Excalibur licked Samuel's hand from his place underneath the table. Then Blanche, whose swept-back blond hair glistened in the overhead lights, spoke up. "This reminds me of a La Fontaine fable."

"What are you talking about, child?" said Melba.

"La Fontaine was a French author of fables. One of them was about a goat that carried a statue in the back of a cart around the streets of a village. The statue was adorned in ancient and very exquisite robes, and it got a lot of attention because of its elegant attire. Over time, the goat took on airs, as if the public were admiring him. The moral of the fable is that it's the robe that's important, not the statue—and certainly not you, a stupid goat!"

They all laughed.

"I like that," said Samuel. "That bastard used his robe to fool the public and obviously thought it would protect him—that it gave him impunity. In the end, however, he was just like a goat putting on airs."

"Imagine all the damage Peterson's abuse of power had on peoples' lives," said Blanche.

"Speaking of current affairs," said Melba. "Whatever happened to Min Fu-Hok?"

"We'll never know," said Samuel, setting his drink down on one of the many rings staining the Round Table. "It won't do any good to ask Mr. Song because he won't talk about it, and when I ask his niece Melody, she just tells me to talk to him."

"There's a mystery for you to solve, Samuel," said Melba.

"I don't think so. I've already tried everything I know. I even asked Barry Fong-Torres to help me, and he hit the same dead end I did. I'll guess I'll just have to leave that one to the powers that be."

Samuel shrugged his shoulders and lifted his glass again. As he did, he caught the bartender's eye. "Give me another Scotch on the rocks."